Copyright © 2021 Penelope Wylde.

All rights reserved.

Edited by Em Petrova

Proofread by Charity Chimni

Cover Design: Bookin' It Designs www.bookinitdesigns.com

No part of this publication may be reproduced, distributed or transmitted in any form or by any means, including photocopying, recording, or other electronic or mechanical methods, without the prior written permission of the publisher, except in the case of brief quotations embodied in critical reviews and certain other noncommercial uses permitted by copyright law. For permission requests, email to authorpenelopewylde@gmail.com

Publisher's Note: This is a work of fiction. Names, characters, places, and incidents are a product of the author's imagination. Locales and public names are sometimes used for atmospheric purposes. Any resemblance to actual people, living or dead, or to businesses, companies, events, institutions, or locales is completely coincidental.

Visit my website at: www.penelopewylde.com

ISBN-13 : 979-8737397807

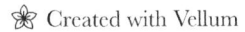

❦ Created with Vellum

MERCY FOR THREE

Second chances come in threes with my brother's best friends.

This was supposed to be a solo healing trip. The plan: return to the mountains, find my way again after we lost my brother. Then move on.

I had everything planned out down to how many bottles of wine it would take. What I never expected was for three irresistible alphas to bust through my door dragging the past in with them.

My brother's three best friends are home on leave, and they have ideas on how they want to spend their furlough and their obsessive attentions are solely on me. Did I picture myself with them when I barely knew what love was? Hell, yes!

What's so bad about falling for three Marines with talented, dirty mouths and hard bodies? They left my heart shattered beyond repair once already. I can't fall for them. Not again.

But their claiming kisses and possessive caresses have me second-guessing my bachelorette status and wondering what letting three men worship me forever could do for a wounded heart.

ONE
MERCY

Moonlight kisses the smooth edges of muscle lined up in front of me. My brother's three best friends stand shoulder to shoulder, forming a forbidden dream package I can't look away from.

Our traditional homecoming celebrations have died down, and I finally have all three alone.

I take a deep breath. Okay. Here goes. *You can do this, Mercy.* I steel my nerves. This is my chance to push for them to see me as the beautiful woman and not the forbidden little sister of a friend.

All three are after different things. Fresh beers and snacks, I imagine, and not expecting me to amble in behind them.

I've given this a lot of thought and I know what I want, so I need to just do it.

I step into the kitchen on bare feet and stop just short of being able to touch Cain's sculpted shoulders and alphalicious ass. Damn, I love a man who can fill out his pair of jeans. Wait.

I'm getting off track. I yank my eyes off the man meat and clear my throat. "I want all three of you to take my virginity." No meshing words, no playing coy. I've done that for years, and I'm no little girl anymore to be hiding behind cute, flirty smiles. I let out a shaky breath. There—I said it, and there's no taking it back. My heart is racing so fast I fear they can hear it thudding heavily in my chest.

Standing in the kitchen of my family's lakeside cabin, every part of me tingles and buzzes as three of the sexiest men I've ever laid eyes on all turn to stare back at me in complete shock, their original mission completely forgotten.

My brother's friends from high school and on into college are long since graduated and now full-fledged Marines with the tats and tags to prove it. Three drool-worthy men with angled jawlines, miles of hard, muscled flesh and intoxicating masculinity with only a tiny kitchen island between us. And a small one at that.

Okay, and well, there's the small detail of my age too, I guess. God forbid I forget that, but I wish *they* would. My fantasies about all three turn filthier the older I get, and at a week before my eighteen birthday, my body can't take *not* having what it wants.

After a second they start to blink but their mouths are still hanging open.

"I've been thinking about it…for…" I swallow past the embarrassment, eyes firmly locked on my folded hands. "…for a long time and I don't know if I can wait any longer." That's not true, entirely. In fact, not at all. I'd wait a lifetime if they asked.

My momma always said I needed a filter between my brain and mouth, but honestly, when has being subtle ever gotten anyone anything they ever wanted? Never is the answer to that question in my experience and when it comes to these men, they've never beat around the bush in the years that I've known them, so I won't either.

"Come again?" Cain chokes out, wiping at the spilled beer running down his chin with a nearby towel.

"The hell…" Grant bangs on Cain's back before his hard, bright blue eyes lock on me. "Not gonna happen. You don't even know what you're asking, little girl," he states, unblinking, and crosses his arms over his bare chest as if the topic is closed.

Beside him, Cain regains his composure, tossing aside the kitchen towel. "What exactly have you been thinking?"

He stalks toward me, his height causing me to crane my neck to keep my gaze locked on his.

I hesitate, sucking my bottom lip between my teeth. Hell of a time to get cold feet, but I can't find it in me to tell them how I've dreamed of tasting each of them on my tongue before taking them with my body.

"Whoa, don't scare the little thing, can't you see she's already shaking?" Lincoln who would usually reach out and pull me in for a hug stands noticeably still. One hand tucked into his jean pocket and the other safely wrapped around a half-empty beer bottle. "Besides," he slips in, "It's not like we haven't thought about it, too," he says all the while looking me in the eye. I follow the head of the bottle to his lips as he raises it, and I wish it were my clit he was sucking on instead of that damn beer.

Both his and Cain's hungry looks have my nipples puckered tight beneath my thin tank top and my thighs clenched together under a matching blue skirt that exposes every inch of my tan legs. Needing all the ammo at my disposal, a lot of thought went into the girly summer outfit I picked out for this evening. Three nights ago my brother called with the news he and the boys would be home on leave. Since my parents took off for Washington state for a business meeting that left me as hostess and as all the times before, this means long nights at the cabin around a bonfire by the lake and cookouts like the one I planned this evening. With graduation a week behind me and my brother off with his sometimes girlfriend, I'm left alone with three very handsome men and my actively dirty mind.

Their expressions turn dark, growing heavy with forbidden desire as I press my thighs a little tighter to stave off the throbbing need they stir inside me. A feeling I don't quite know how to control or ease just yet, but I'm hoping they'll help me learn.

"I've heard the rumors. Everyone has. I know you like to share your lovers." I raise my eyes to touch each of them. As much as it hurts to know they've had other lovers, they've never done anything in front of me, but I hear the whispers and see the dreamy looks in some of the girls' eyes when I'm in town.

"Rumors, huh?"

My eyes flick over to Lincoln's with a haughty glare. "Girls talk down at the pub. I have ears, ya know. You can't just blow into town while on leave, have a little fun, and not expect the ladies to talk." Everyone gathers there to have a steak dinner and catch the town news and "the boys" were the main topic more than once.

"Don't believe everything you hear, Mercy, baby."

My eyes narrow on the more muscled of the three. "You don't need to coddle me, Cain. I'm a big girl now and you don't need to protect me from the truth. And none of that changes how I feel. I know what I want." I slip in there while I have all three of their undivided attention.

"Don't encourage her, dammit," Grant runs a frustrated hand through his hair. "She doesn't need any more ideas put into her pretty head."

Grant's the older of the three by a few months, and he thinks that makes his word the final word, and well, he has another think coming because I didn't come here to take no for an answer.

Anyone with eyes knows I've crushed on all three men since I was a fresh-faced fourteen-year-old who didn't understand the feelings and emotions running through her body for one man much less three. And now that I'm older I know what my body wants, and it's screaming to have all three touch me, lick me and take me in ways that will leave me ruined for any other man. Once I set my mind on something, it will take a hurricane stronger than what this world has ever seen to change me from my course.

My hand flies to my hair and I loosen the pencil I have holding my long wall of blonde hair away from my face in a messy bun. Wavy curls tumble over my shoulders and down my back, making them all groan and give away what they're really thinking.

But if not for that little slip, you wouldn't know it from the stone-cold face Grant wears like a safety mask against me and what it seems he wants to hide. "Forget it, Mercy. Your tight, sweet ass isn't getting anywhere near our dicks. That's a promise." His words are constricted if not a little forced like he is fighting against every single syllable.

As he talks, he grabs another beer from the fridge and leans his half-naked body against the counter, giving me a full view of all that tight, hard muscle and the dark dustings of a treasure trail I want to run my tongue over.

My gaze drops to the obvious hard-on bulging from between his legs. I don't know a lot of things when it comes to sex, but I do know what *that* means.

Heat of the summer has them stripped down to jeans only and my inexperience sends a flush of scarlet over my cheeks as I drink in their golden, ripped flesh. The popped buttons and low ride of those jeans don't go unappreciated either.

"Yep. What he said." Cain claps a hand over Grant's shoulder, pointing his beer at me. "Jail bait, sweetheart. That's what you are no matter how fuckable that sweet body is. Can't happen." I could always count on Cain telling me the truth while making me feel good. He never did like hurting my feelings and took extra care to protect me.

Being super shy, I never could summon the courage to approach any of them until tonight. Why? Because my time with them is running out. I always flirted and played around with the three of them when they visited. Stolen glances and warm hugs and a few kisses on the cheek here and there have fueled fantasies of something more for at least me, but as I turn to look at Lincoln standing quietly to the side, peering down at me with that dark, broody look of his, I finally realize something. Everything that I feel, and desire, is not all one-sided. They want this as much as I do. Question is, what will it take to push them over the edge and claim me?

"What exactly do you want from us, Mercy, when you drop something like that in our laps?" Linc finally finds his voice and it's as raw as I feel.

I hope to push them into at least admitting they feel something for me. But my inexperience shines through again as I stay quiet, and my heart crumbles little by little as none of them make a move. For once I should have listened to my mother and not be so damn headstrong. I go to turn, but it's Lincoln who draws me up short.

I clench my jaw to fight back the hurt and tears. "This was a mistake. I definitely shouldn't have come on to any of you. I'm sorry."

"Aww…son of a bitch, come here, baby." Lincoln passes his beer to Grant and takes me in his arms, pulling me into his warm chest, and I nuzzle deep into his hold. "It's not like that, Mercy. Just be patient." His arms are around me, holding me tight, and it takes my lust-craving mind to realize he's picked me up and I have my legs wrapped around his waist. The heat of his bulge pressing against my bare, starving vagina.

He pulls me up to face him, and I lean forward to rest my forehead against his, our breathing hard and shallow. "I don't know how to control what I'm feeling inside," I whisper, digging my hands into his hair. "It burns and aches and all I know is that when I see you, all three of you, it goes away and I can finally breathe again."

"My God," he says and then his lips are on mine hungrily. A burst of flavor from his beer hits my tongue, and I'm suddenly more ravenous than I've ever been. I groan, tightening my hold around his neck and melting into him as he drags his tongue over mine.

Another hand comes to rest on my lower back, and I'm melting into the wall of heat replacing it as Grant moves my hair to the side and pulls me back to rest against his chest. Spread between him and Linc, he takes the soft lobe of my ear between his lips and sucks.

Shock from the sudden burst of pleasure tightens my legs around Linc and I try to move against his hard length, but a firm grip on my hips keeps me still. "What do you have on under that skimpy little skirt you've been teasing us with all day? Thong, silk, lace…" Grant's voice is gravelly as he runs the tip of his finger along the band of my skirt.

I lick my kiss-swollen lips, still tasting Linc and before I can give an answer, another hand is on the back of my head, turning me. "Cain," I say softly and his mouth is on mine. He's just as claiming and heated as Linc, but there's something slower about the way he glides his tongue over my lips, teasing them open before he enters my mouth.

"Wrong on all accounts," I pant, breaking away from Cain's kiss and catching Linc's gaze. "I'm not wearing any panties."

Linc shifts, and I know that's when he realizes I have my bare pussy against his jeans, dry humping his thick cock.

Grant digs his fingers into my hair and turns my head. "You're asking for trouble. You're like wild, raw fire…you'll be the death of us all."

In all the moving and tugging, my tank has ridden high and so has my skirt, I notice. I close my eyes and circle my hips over Linc's hard length and marvel in the feel of Cain's firm, warm lips kissing my exposed midriff just below the heavy ampleness of my breasts.

Enjoying the pleasure of his touch, I work hard to convince my body it's okay to breathe every few seconds or risk passing out and missing all their gentle touching and delicious kisses.

Slowly, I ease my hand over Cain's and guide him higher, only to hear a rasping *fuck* fall from his lips, but he doesn't stop me.

ONE

I moan as strong fingers work and knead the soft flesh, and my nipples scream to be pinched, tugged and sucked. I let my head drop back onto Grant's shoulder and reach around to bury my hands in his hair, wanting to feel more of him…of…of…I don't know, just more.

Cain massages and twists the tight tips of my breasts between his fingers, and that's all it takes to help take the edge off.

"You like that Mercy, baby?"

Linc's cock twitches at Cain's question, and I groan my answer as girl cream slips from my slit to wet my thighs and his pants. Without a word, I hold Cain and Linc's gazes as I edge my pink-tipped fingers down my curves to bury in the soft cotton of my skirt. Inch by inch, I raise the material until the pink, wet flesh of my pussy peeks out from beneath the lacy ruffles.

All three men's nostrils flare, and I see their massive chests expand as they inhale the scent of my arousal.

"Touch me," I beg to any one of them who will put me out of my misery. "I need to feel your hands all over me, on me…in me!"

This was no game and no going back from here. Grant is supporting half my weight against his chest, leaving his hands free to roam. He strokes both thumbs in the seam of my thighs, but never touches my greedy vagina.

This is beyond crazy.

Grant blows out a hiss of air, his head hanging a moment before he drags his eyes up my body to find mine. "Fuck, baby, your little virgin pussy is all dripping wet and perfectly bare."

"Did you do that for *us*?" Cain asks.

"Isn't that what you like…?" I swallow thickly. "Don't you like your women bare for you? Do you like what you see?"

Cain grabs me by the hips, stroking tiny mind-blowing circles across the area right above my hips bone. I moan, clawing at his shoulders, pulling his lips closer to where I need him, but he's obviously in control, and I can't budge him, and each caress is like a tease of what he's not giving me.

With my skirt around my waist and breasts exposed, Linc holds me up with the help of Cain and kneels between my spread thighs.

"Please God, give us the strength," Linc murmurs. Two large hands spread me wide, parting my ass cheeks and exposing every part of me to all of them. "Liking is our problem. You're too fucking young for the three of us," he says, and I can hear the pain in Linc's voice and see the war raging behind those dark chocolate eyes of his.

"God, baby, this is so wrong. So beautiful." His eyes are filled with fury, not for me, but for himself. Yet instead of pulling away, he leans in, dragging his thick, warm tongue in the V of my thigh, teasing me higher and higher into an orgasm floating just beyond my reach. If only he would rub my clit, eat me, finger me… "Ohhh!" …just *something*!

I groan with a fresh wave of frustration. "Linc, please," I beg. My pussy throbs and I rock my hips, desperate to feel them there. Realizing he's not going to touch me, I slip my hand down my body and dip my finger into my soaked hole and bring it back to circle my clit.

"Ahh," I gasp, clenching my thighs, but Linc's massive shoulders have me pinned wide open.

"Faster," Linc instructs, and I follow his command.

I buck and scream, feeling the inevitable sizzling in every nerve ending in my body.

Through my tank top, Cain pinches both my nipples and Grant turns my head, claiming my mouth just as I scream from the sudden flash of pleasure that shoots through me.

Hot, sticky cum spills from my virgin slit to drench my pouty lips and thighs. I mutter a stream of incoherent rumblings, unable to focus through so much pleasure and the taste of Grant in my mouth.

"That's it, baby." Cain nuzzles me on my other side as Grant firmly holds me in place in his arms.

Grant breaks our kiss and gently runs his fingers over my face. "So beautiful."

Ragged breaths tear from me, and it takes long moments before I can manage to open my eyes.

"That was…was…sooooo good," I finally manage around a grin.

Lost in the moment, I don't realize Linc has settled my feet back on the floor until he steps away, pulling my skirt down and smoothing it over my hips.

"Beautiful and perfect." There's something distant in his tone that has my heart flying and not in a good way.

"What's going on? Why are you stopping?"

Just like that, the atmosphere in the small kitchen shifts from scorching hot to freezing cold.

"Did I do something wrong?" My gaze flicks between the men. Linc across the small kitchen and Grant and Cain by my side, slowly withdrawing to leave me standing alone.

"We'd ruin you, our sweet Mercy. Do you have any idea of how twisted we fucking are, little girl? Of what we would demand of you? Want you to do to us? For us?" His voice grows increasingly agitated. "This can never happen again."

He turns from me and stalks across the kitchen before he's back at my side, chest heaving.

"Yes. That's what I want," I say looking up at him, hoping I sound as convincing as I feel. "I know exactly what I'm asking." But his smirk tells me he sees through my bravado.

Behind me, Grant scrubs a hand down his face, but he hasn't pulled completely away. Not yet. I turn in his arms, and Cain moves in, taking Linc's place. "He's right. We do this and it will fuck us all up and for good. Then there's your brother. If he knew what we just did, we wouldn't have to worry about getting KIA—he'd do the job single-handed."

I can't believe what I'm hearing. What the heck is happening here? "Since when are you guys chicken? You barely touched me and now you're going to walk away?"

Grant steps back a few paces, and with each foot he put between us, another layer of shields springs back up after I spent the last half-hour knocking them down. "We shouldn't have even done that much. Look—your brother is going to be back with his girlfriend any second."

I turn to Cain, my voice choking with the amount of lust I have dripping through my body thanks to them. "One orgasm? Is that all I get and just like that I'm trash? No good?"

Cain is by my side, running the back of his knuckles down my cheek. "Don't ever talk about yourself that way."

I rise to the tips of my toes, pressing my palms against his hard pecs. "I move that zipper down a little and I'll find an angry, hard cock thirsty for my juices, won't I?" I whisper in his ear before pulling back.

"You're playing a game you don't know how to play, little girl."

"Then teach me, touch me. Just don't leave me like this… wanting and aching. I need you." I take a breath, turn my head enough where I can look each of them in the eye and say the truth. "All of you."

"Silence, woman. Wanting you is the worst possible idea."

Grant's words are more gargled hisses through clenched teeth than actual talking, and the bulging tendons in his neck tell me he's about to snap. But it's the other bulge that has my attention. Jeans can't hide that massive hard dick any better than my thumb can hide the sun.

His eyes darken, flashing over me.

My gaze falls to his lips.

"Look at me," he gruffly commands, and I purr with a little shiver.

I drag my gaze up his bare chest and whimper from the fiery need I see there in his eyes. But I also see anger glitter in those depths, and the fine lines of control he's exerting over himself ripple through the deeply contoured muscles.

Holy fucking hotness.

I moan quietly, but I know he hears it.

Grant's nostrils flare, and he growls like a beast edging out all the sensual pleasure I saw there a moment ago.

The room draws uncomfortably quiet. "What the hell just happened. You guys act like you weren't doing exactly what I wanted."

When I think my heart can't take another hit, Linc pushes past us and walks out the screen door, making me jump when it slams shut behind him.

"Go the fuck upstairs, Mercy, and lock the fucking door for the night."

I can't move, can't believe what I am hearing much less convince my feet to obey.

Grant roars and brings his fist down on the marble with a loud thud. "Now, Mercy."

My eyes go wide when I see a fracture run down the middle of the black and gray marble.

"Grant, Cain—" My voice is a hollow, rasp. I don't know what they need me to do to make this okay for them, but I'll try anything.

Grant turns his fiery blue eyes on me, shaking his head. "You have my word this will never happen again. We leave in the morning, honey. Another tour that will take us from here so you can have a normal life."

I don't believe what I am hearing. My gaze flashes between Cain's and Grant's, confused as the room draws uncomfortably quiet.

Only a single word he said registers. *Leaving.*

"Don't go. Stay. For me." I reach for them, turning to see Linc outside looking in.

"You know we can't. You're too innocent and young for what we want."

Cain turns and comes to stand in front of me. "Please forgive us. We didn't mean to take advantage of you. One too many beers maybe, but... fuck it. Like Grant said, this will never happen again. You have all three of our promises."

Grant leans into me and places a tender kiss on my forehead, and it feels like the seal of death. "We shouldn't have come here. Being alone with you was too damn tempting and we caved."

With that, both men turn from me, and I watch their retreating backs fade into the darkness, taking my heart with them. That's the last time I saw them but not the last time my heart shatters into a million jagged pieces.

TWO

MERCY, SEVEN YEARS LATER

"I'm doing this, Mom. Don't worry about me. I'll be fine. It's not like I'm going off-grid forever or running away to some nudist colony off planet."

She gives a long sigh I've come to recognize as the patient version. "You were always the stubborn one. Be careful. No one has been up there since before your brother. There's a long pause and a deep sigh before my mom continues, and I feel the break in her words and the unspoken emotion that went behind it like it were my own. "I don't like the idea of you all alone is all I'm saying. What if some crazy loon has broken in? You'd be all alone."

Highly doubtful since everyone knows everyone in the small lakeside community the size of a shoebox, but that doesn't seem to deter the woman. "I've taken care of myself for the last six and a half years and have lived in four different countries, Mom. I think I can handle a little cabin in the woods in Upstate New York. Stop worrying. I'll call you later and let you know if I find any crazy person growing potatoes for moonshine in our bathtub. Love ya bunches. I have to go now."

If I let her continue, there will never be an end to the "what if'" questions. Ever since my brother died, all she does is worry, which causes me to worry and I already have enough anxiety issues without taking on hers. But I know she does it out of love, so I try to keep it light. "Then again, if our pretend moonshiner has some good stuff…" I let my words trail off as my mom's soft laughter fills my ear.

"Moonshine or not, just because you've traveled to a few countries doesn't mean something can't happen; remember that, honey. Now, your dad had the power and water turned back on, but I don't think he was happy about it." Which was code for I'd be getting a call from him later to check in on me.

"Give him a big kiss for me and know I love you guys," I say.

"Okay. We love you too, babe. Talk soon."

There is an odd note to the way she says "okay" that tells me I haven't heard the last of this, but I shrug it off as I end the call and toss the phone in the passenger side of my rental car. I hit the button to lower the window and breathe in a lungful of fresh mountain air.

I've missed this place more than I realized. Beautiful towering pines and lush oaks decades older than my quarter of a century have my attention. Each twist and bow in the wind welcoming me as I slow my car. I'd forgotten how beautiful this place is in the summertime.

I flick on the signal light and make a left down a long, uneven and neglected dirt path tucked away and completely hidden from the main road.

In the distance I see glittering waters sparkle through the hanging branches in the early afternoon sun. I feel like I've rediscovered a forbidden hideaway as I pull to a stop outside the two-story log cabin my family inherited from my great-grandparents around the time my brother was born.

The scent of pine and sweet honeysuckle hits me first, and then I notice a storm hanging out over the distant mountains that will probably greet me around dinnertime.

"Maybe I am off planet," I mutter to myself as I kill the engine, because even overgrown, this place has a magic about it. Such a stark contrast to the congested hustle of New York City I'm used to.

No other soul is in sight and only the soft calling of a distant owl and the rustle of wind through the leaves can be heard as I step from the car and make my way around to the other side to pluck up my box of provisions. I gather the neatly packed box and prop it under an arm and head for the large porch.

I thought about the last time I ran my hand over this exact spot of the polished railing. The last time I sat around the warm campfire sharing stories with family and friends down by the lake.

Images of Linc, Cain and Grant flow in and out of my mind as they often do, but they seem stronger, more vivid standing here where they spent so much of their time with us.

It's been far too long. Seven years now. Most of that I spent off at college and then pursuing a career in writing children's books and illustrations that has kept me busy and content for the most part.

I stayed away because of them and what happened between us that night. Before I could find my way back, my brother was killed in action. That happened over a year and a half ago, and after that, my heart couldn't take the thought of coming here and not seeing him.

TWO

Everyone said to give it time, but I'm tired of hurting and can't help but wonder if I'll ever be happy again. The several unfinished manuscripts on my hard drive are a testament to that. I have a steady clientele who keep me from going hungry, but my passion is drier than the Mojave.

The tears have stopped coming every night but standing outside the door looking out over the one place on earth he loved with all his heart, I feel them stinging the back of my eyes. His slice of heaven has become the one place neither my parents nor I can bear visiting and because of that, here I stand.

Balancing the box of goods on one hip, I run the tips of my fingers over the once gleaming polished wood time has faded into a dull brown instead of its once lustrous chestnut.

Unlike the memories I have of my last time here. Those have not faded by any stretch as I cup my hand around my eyes to peek through the side kitchen window.

A new agony pierces my heart even as excitement at being here again fills me. But I'm not here for the men I once thought I loved.

I roll my eyes at my inner thoughts. Of course, my head wants to go there. Although in my defense, it is easier to think about them than my brother.

I take the porch steps two at a time, breathing in the warm air. Summer is in full swing with the occasional dragonfly or grasshopper doing their thing in the vast yard that lies between the cabin and lake.

Guilt at abandoning the once beautiful spot eats away at me and my heart grows heavy, but I'm here now. And with a plan. I just need to step back, clear my head long enough to let my heart find some kind of inner peace. I'm here to give myself a chance at rediscovering what I love most, or I'm going to sink like a boulder. It's a freaking miracle I haven't already. Luckily, I have a fabulous agent who's helped me land good contracts that have earned me a shit ton of money, but it's not going to be long before that dries up. Plus, I'm on a deadline to deliver a finished manuscript in three weeks.

I almost feel guilty I haven't started, but what can I say? I've hit a brick wall and my heart just isn't in it anymore.

So I'm going to take a page out of my own book for once, purge my soul and sweat it out the old-fashioned way.

If I can't, it will cost me everything.

No more writing or painting for young hearts.

No more career.

Not that I have much of one at the moment anyway, but I'd like to salvage something before my agent drops me.

I slip in the key my dad reluctantly gave me a few days ago, step inside and immediately feel the dry emptiness. Once quaint and homey, the bare walls of the wide-open layout lack signs anyone ever lived here. Framed pictures have been put away, no plants to speak of. All the dust and sheet-covered furniture don't help either. Upstairs there are three bedrooms that won't be much different.

I knew what to expect before I even started the long drive here, so I steel my nerves and refuse to let myself fall back into the big rabbit hole staring back at me, big and ugly as it is.

To the left is the kitchen. I place the box down on the counter, take in the filth and feel a sudden stab of depression. Because of the lack of attention to the place, but more so because there's nothing here and I am all alone.

"You wanted this, so suck it up."

Okaaay. I take a deep breath. Kitchen is the heart of a home, my mom always said, so I start there. Cleaning away the dust and plugging in the slightly outdated fridge is the first order of business. Besides the sandwiches I picked up at a small diner along the way, I didn't bring any perishables. Just dried fruits, granola, canned vegetables and wine. I am a city girl, after all, who likes—okay loves—her wine and preferably chilled. I won't be here long enough to need anything else.

After a few hours, a couple of broken nails and a fat, pulsing blister on my palm, I stand back to take in my handiwork. I've done away with the musty sheets covering the sofas and swept and scrubbed the floors until they gleam.

I take out my phone and snap a quick picture for mom with the caption: "No ax murderers found, just killer floors" with a heart emoji and hit send.

My tattered jeans and faded Aerosmith T-shirt is dirtier than the cabin, so that says something of a job well done, but… err…it's not perfect. The large front windows still need a wipe down and the overgrown yard is still cringe-worthy, but I'd rather not think about all the tangled weeds outside when I have my own to tend to.

I put away all the cleaning supplies and slip the three bottles of wine into the cooled fridge and one more in the freezer for after my sweating session. Hey, don't judge. I'm twenty miles from the nearest store and half that from any neighbor. Can't blame a girl for bringing backups.

I run out to the car for my bags and another box filled with candles as the storm moves in on a low rumble.

Perfect.

Ten minutes later, I step from the bathroom freshly showered, tucking the end of my towel between my breasts. I neatly fold my dirty clothes and pack away the bottles of shampoo and lotions before I pad my way downstairs. There is wood and the necessary kindling for a fire stacked by the fireplace from someone's last trip here and within a few minutes, I have a nice blaze heating the entire place.

Next is the incense. I pull several packets from my box and little stands that fit several sticks of Magnolia for peace and lilac for soothing the soul. Or so said the kind lady in the incense shop. She's given me a wand of sage too, just to cover all bases, I assume. She kept looking at the dark circles under my eyes and *tsking* at me. Who am I to argue?

A few people gawked at me when I piled half of the shop's candle stock into my cart, but as I place them around the cabin and others in a large circle in the middle of the living room, I find their warming glow soothing.

Oh yeah, I can feel my soul starting to stir. This just might work after all.

Satisfied, I drape my towel over a chair and come to stand in the middle of my circle of candles. Not another soul around, I remind myself and then fall into warrior's pose. Hold. Another five minutes and I dip into a sun salutation, stretching out all the kinks from the long drive while the strain heats my muscles.

I push back into downward dog and hold. Sweat pebbles over my skin and I let my eyes drift closed.

A loud bang from behind me shatters my calm.

TWO

My eyes fling open as the lights flicker from a crack of lightning.

I peer through my open legs, every inch of my naked ass in the air, to see the upside-down face of a man.

My heart wants to stop mid-beat. My lungs, however, are working overtime and I'm about to pass out.

"Mercy, baby? What the hell are you doing?"

THREE
MERCY

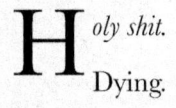

H*oly shit.*
Dying.

That is what I am doing.

This can't be happening.

I drop my head between my legs and take another look at the man standing in my doorway.

Oh crap. It is.

My heart swings around my ears.

Grant is checking out my ass. Grant *fucking* Cross is standing in my door checking out my *ass!*

And he's not alone.

Breathe.

On the outside, I'm fighting to keep it all cool like I always do my yoga out in the middle of nowhere naked with the door unlocked in a ring of candles and incense. Err…okay, this probably looks like I'm summoning hell's wrath right now, but my home…my rules.

In hindsight, I shoulda locked the door.

Blood shoots to my face, and I'm beet red by the time I gain enough sense to get my ass out of the air and stand up.

On the inside, it's a whole other story. I'm the freaked-out girl in the middle of a nightmare walking into the school gym butt-ass naked and everyone gawking at me.

Yeah, but being the overachiever that I am, what I think I should do turns into another problem, when my fumbling to stand causes my round, heavy tits to sway. Their sharp gazes hone in on my blushing puckered nipples like starving men to ripe fruit.

I thought I'd forgotten how gorgeous all three of my brother's best friends were, but Jesus help me I was wrong. The image in my mind hasn't faded a bit, but it also doesn't do them justice either. Time and the harsh life of the military has aged them into warriors and not in a bad way either.

In the past I would have run to Cain and thrown my arms around his neck and greeted him with a big kiss. And then worked down the line until all three felt warm and welcomed home. But that was a long time ago.

I plant my feet to the floor and ignore the grin working its way across Grant's face.

Grant's rich, brown hair has a faint brushing of silver along the front but his captivating, royal blue eyes are sharp and don't miss a thing. Age has only made the man more rugged and all the hotter, I notice.

And so does my body, when a flush of warmth fills me.

Those eyes are trained on me. Midnight dark one minute and light as the sky the next like he can't decide on what mood he wants to settle on—excited or pissed off that I'm here. His jeans wrap around perfect thighs and his green military-issued T-shirt stretches across rippling, tanned muscle that makes me thirsty just looking at him. He could be red carpet material with little effort.

His jaw is clenched tight as he takes in every exposed inch of my body. Those strong hands of his are filled with an array of bags carrying God knows what. Probably a lifetime supply of batteries and coffee if memories serve. My brother always joked Grant never left home unprepared and he was the man you always wanted at your back.

Apparently, that is still true.

From across the room I see a dark flash of something in those once familiar eyes, but the connection is severed when Cain shoulders past Grant with the same surprised look that seems stuck in place for the last several minutes.

A gray beanie is pulled over hair I remember as dark as midnight on a moonless night.

I'm not sure what they expected when they walked in here. It is my cabin, after all. I mean, I guess my bare ass was a surprise, but oh well.

Anyway.

I clench my back teeth in frustration and force a harsh breath out.

Something shared between them has me shivering in the dead of summer in front of a lit fireplace, and I feel it like a wicked caress between my thighs. That *something* is only the feel of old

THREE

memories, I tell myself. In a surprise turn of events my heart tends to agree with my brain for once.

I'm instantly taken back to the night in the kitchen with Cain teasing me into an orgasm and Grant and Lincoln refusing to touch me where I needed them most to alleviate the pain.

The trek back into the past lasts all of a second and then reality bursts over us, drowning out the heat and swirling me back into my current predicament.

"What are you guys stopping in the door for? This isn't some lightweight crap I'm lugging. Grant has everything but the fucking chainsaw in here. Get out of the door already."

Lincoln pushes through the wall of muscles blocking my doorway only to come to a complete standstill alongside his friends, all but pinning me to the wall with his dark stare.

They're huge, taking up the double-wide doorway with Cain an inch or two shorter than the others, but he's stacked like a linebacker. They all are. If I still thought like the teenage girl I was once upon a time, I'd say it was one of the reasons I first felt attracted to them. But I've grown past that, but yeah, the eye candy is still appreciated.

My breasts heave with my deep breaths and that stirs up more than any of us expect, from the bulges in their jeans. My eyes land there, and I don't hide the fact either.

"Boys. Decide to drop in for a visit, huh?"

I don't know what exactly has me coming up with that corny line, but I draw it out slowly like I'm the very epitome of sexy. And okay as far as lines go that earns at least a five since it was totally on the fly. I'm working with an empty barrel here, no judging.

None of that changes the fact I'm facing two choices. Flail around and pretend they haven't seen me at least mostly naked already and make a mad dash for my towel halfway across the room or let them stare at all my curves and dips.

Since I'll probably trip over every single candle on my way to my towel and then burn down the whole freaking place, I pin my shoulders back and tilt my chin high with the last drop of pride I can muster.

"Are we interrupting anything?"

Lincoln asks the obvious as he scans every inch of the place. When he doesn't find anything—or anyone—his gaze swings over my body and dips to find my freshly waxed folds.

Lincoln might not be the take-charge kind of guy Grant is, but that doesn't keep him from stepping out front of the group. "Well?" he asks in a challenging tone as if I owe him an explanation for being naked in my own living room.

"Well, what?" I level back, crossing my arms over my bare breasts. I keep eye contact as all three push deeper into the cabin.

"Are you alone?" he huffs.

"Find out for yourself." I can't tell who my words piss off more. Cain, the most laid back of the trio or Lincoln who doesn't like surprises.

I saunter by them, heading for the stairs and I hear three long, hard inhales. I know each of them smells the new soap of lavender and honey I used and I kind of like knowing they're getting all hot and bothered even if I don't know why they are standing in the middle of my doorway just yet.

And that is how it all starts. The thrilling, exciting scariest new chapter of my life.

Hells fire!

I can feel their eyes stroking over the soft jiggle of my ass with each step I take.

Just three more steps.

Two.

One loud thud on the floor tells me they've dropped all their boxes in unison. Then I hear the front door slam.

Are they following me? Did they leave?

Before I duck around the corner, the urge to look over my shoulder has me turning. I wish I could play a better game because the look in Grant's eyes tells me that one move lost me the game.

But what his heated gaze doesn't tell me is why all three are standing in the middle of my living room to begin with.

FOUR
GRANT

Not much fazes me, but I'm utterly stunned into silence when I push open the front door to find Mercy bent over, legs locked and ass thrust in the air.

My heart was already pounding at the thought of seeing our girl again the whole drive up here, but what I walk into has my dick turning into solid steel and no way my heart has a chance in hell of recovering.

The girl we knew was beautiful and a cock tease for sure, but from all the angles greeting us now—and damn those are some juicy curves—our best friend's little sis has turned into a peach of a woman. Ripe and finally ready for the taking.

She stands, her long, blonde hair fanning over her shoulders and back in a wavy mess that has me holding my breath.

I take a quick once over of the room and note there's only a single bottle of water on a side table. Not two. And one towel on the back of the chair with no stray pair of men's shoes to be seen by the front door.

FOUR

Good. I didn't want to have to bury my fist in some guy's face and freak Mercy out even more than she already is.

When her mother called us a few days ago with a favor to ask, there was no mention of a man in her daughter's life, but one never knows. Of course, once we heard the favor was for Mercy, none of us hesitated. We have another two weeks on our furlough and we all agreed this was the best use of our time. Hell, it's been forever, since we've returned and seeing the place again does my soul good and I know the same goes for the guys.

But seeing her is even better.

That truth is written all over our faces.

We've been thinking on this day since we had to walk away from her and now that we have her in the middle of nowhere with nothing—and no one—between us, we're not letting her go.

We all know Mercy is still hurting over the loss of her brother. Her mom has kept us in the loop and we've reached out to her when not out on missions. But circumstances always kept us from coming home and our girl has a bit of a travel bug in her given this is the first time she's stepping on U.S. soil since her brother's funeral. Otherwise, this little reunion would have happened a long time before now.

It took a lot of restraint from all of us, but we gave her space. We've been away long enough and it's time to set a few things straight.

A short talk over a large bottle of tequila made all three of us realize our girl needs a little TLC so she can move on and find happiness again. From the haughty look in her eyes, she might need a spanking on that fine ass of hers to go along with the kisses we intend on lavishing her with once we get past the hard part.

Talking to us.

Jesting aside, we can only hope she's ready for her future to include the three of us because we're not leaving here until we have her fully claimed by three perverted kinky motherfuckers who want her like we've wanted no other woman.

Refusing her that night was the best and worst day of all our lives. We had to walk away, which killed each of us, but we also had the knowledge that one day maybe she would take all three of us. And that kept us alive out on the battlefield more than I care to think about, really. There were a lot of close calls.

The second her sweet ass disappears from view we all three drop our heavy loads, and I scrub a hand over the short strands of my hair.

I spend a few seconds regaining my thoughts, but Cain recovers before I do.

"Damn," he hisses. "I wish I had more to say to that, but I think I lost some important brain cells." He looks around the cabin and sees what I do. A whole bunch of nothing. A shell of a home compared to what it used to be.

"I thought I was prepared to see that pretty face of hers in person again, but you're right, Cain. Damn." Lincoln claps Cain on the shoulder. "Ya know, from the surprised look on her face and the blush across her ass, I think Mrs. Bray is having a little fun at our expense by not telling her we were coming."

I chuckle, kicking the door closed behind me. "Wouldn't be the first time she's tried to play interference with her kids," I offer, recalling a time Mercy's mother tried to set up our friend with Lincoln's much older, reckless, batshit crazy cousin. Given Linc

FOUR

likes to have control over his surroundings of the three of us, watching that play out made the last year of college interesting.

Watching the much younger version of Mercy get all worked up over nothing was even more so.

"Let's get these to the kitchen and get settled. We can go from there." I bend and grab the first bags of groceries and leave the boxes of batteries, pans and bug repellant to the guys. From what Mrs. Bray told us, her daughter probably didn't come prepared, and from the looks of it, the older woman was right.

So we did.

Cain walks in behind me and slings a couple of boxes onto the counter, and Lincoln is on his heels with a few more bags. Meats, fruits, vegetables and anything else the man jammed in the cart is being pulled out of the bags and laid out.

"Wait. What? Settled. You're not staying here."

Mercy's voice reaches us before she does. She moves quickly down the back stairs leading straight into the kitchen from the second floor. Great for late-night snacks *and* eavesdropping. She shuffles around an amused Linc and Cain to come face to face with me looking flushed and as pissed off as a kicked rattlesnake.

I turn to face her.

She's covered her beautiful body with some sort of ugly sagging sweats the color of moss and an oversized T-shirt with boss babe written over her tits, but I don't think it has the "I'm in control" effect she's going for. More like cute and edible.

I lift my hand and tuck a stray curl of hair behind her ear where she prefers to keep it. "Yeah, as in putting out that blazing fire you have roaring in the middle of the summer, killing all the candles so we don't all die of vanilla overload, figuring out who is sleeping where, making sure the food is secured, then making sure there are no leaks from the storm."

The longer I talk the redder she becomes.

From the other side of the small kitchen island Linc tosses several packs of meats on the counter and says, "I've got the fire." Linc points at Cain who is stowing away the pots and pans. "You?"

"Oh no." I turn to see Mercy hold a hand up like a stop sign in front of Linc before Cain can answer. "Don't you touch my fire *or* my candles!" She bolts across the kitchen and stands in front of the arched doorway, hands on her hips.

My lips jerk back into a smile at the challenge.

And I know what the smirk on Cain's face means. "I'll get the leaks *and* the candles," he says. "Wouldn't want to burn the place down with us in it, right, Mercy baby?" he offers with a wink.

I stand back and cross my arms. Wrong move.

From the way her scowl deepens and those perfectly tweezed brows knit together at hearing Cain's old nickname for her, I'd say if Cain isn't careful, he might find himself sleeping on the front porch.

I watch as she glares at him all the while both men stalk forward, wrap their arms around her and dive in for a quick kiss before moving her to the side.

Kicked rattlesnake or not, I see her ire calm the second Linc swoops in and kisses those perfect lips and then passes her to Cain.

And she kisses them back.

"That's not fair," she huffs at their retreating backs before turning those pretty blues back to me.

And now we're alone.

She stalks forward, a plan clearly in mind. "They don't fight fair and you can get any idea you might have of following in their footsteps out of your head. I don't need my fire killed or my candles snuffed out. What I want to know is why you're here?" She rounds the kitchen island and I can tell she's gunning for the box I'm emptying.

Undeterred, I grab a few bottles of water from the boxes of supplies and turn to open the refrigerator and then freeze. I'm left a little speechless at what I find. Or rather what I don't.

"Nothing but wine and water?" I reach in. "Is that a deli sandwich?"

I turn to look at her and see she's hot on my ass, putting the bottles of steak sauce and plates I've unpacked right back into the boxes I'm trying to unload them from.

She waves a hand in front of my face. "Don't worry about what is and isn't in my fridge. Not your problem. And there's no way you're staying and neither are your two goons for friends."

She plucks the bottles of water from my hands and tosses them back in, and that's when I catch the soft hint of vanilla still clinging to her from all those damn candles she had lit.

She shoots me a humorless grin. "There ya go. You're all packed again. Better get going before the rain floods the roads."

I cock a half smile, causing the pink flush across her cheeks to turn a deep rose. She might think she is in control, but the little spitfire has no idea we've come with a plan in mind. No matter how much she huffs and puffs.

I shake my head and take my box from her hands. "Mercy, that's not gonna happen," I say and snatch the bottles back and pass them to Cain who walks through the door.

One thing about Mercedes Bray is that she likes to be in control. Something we have in common and we've butted heads over in the past. Knocking her off-kilter is the first order of business.

Her long-winded sigh, tells me she's resigned enough to know we are not budging and her hard shell is starting to crack. "Fine. How long are you guys staying?"

"That depends on how long you are staying."

"What does that have to do with anything?"

I close the fridge and prop my hands on the countertop. Cain and Linc standing off to the side in silence. Fuckers. Leaving me to do all the dirty work. "Everything actually."

She tilts her head up and puts on one of those smiles that says she's about to read us the law and blanks her expression. Scary as fuck. I've never seen someone totally erase any trace of emotion that fast. "Then your stay is going to be very short-lived," she coos, and doesn't she sound so smug?

She turns, arms crossed and climbs the stairs, but I'm right behind waving a hand to the guys to give me a minute.

Upstairs I find her in the first room on the left taking clothes from the drawers and neatly folding them into an overnight bag. She's a blur of green and white going back and forth.

I lean a shoulder on the frame of the door and cross my arms. "Where do you think you're going?" I point at those weird-looking pants. "The crotch of those pants is around your knees, for god's sake, woman. You'll trip over something before you make it to your car."

"We can't all be Rambo ready like you are, Grant. My pajamas are none of your concern. And since you refuse to leave, I'm getting out of here before the rain floods my way out."

Like hell she is.

"Really and then what? Drive the four hours back to the city?"

She turns those blazing blue eyes on me, and my heart wants to hit the fucking floor she's so damn beautiful. "Wherever I want to, thank you very much."

"You don't want to give me a hug? Where's my hello kiss? Don't I get one of those anymore?"

She stumbles on her way back from the bathroom, and I reach a hand out to steady her. As insignificant as it might seem, throwing her off balance finally reveals a few cracks along that tough exterior enough to get her to stop and see me for the first time since walking through the front door. Me and not the past.

"It's been a while since I've seen you. Why don't you get over here and wrap those sweet arms around me?" My voice pitches low. "I've missed you, sweetheart."

It's the truth. Seeing her makes all the emotions I shoved down to do my job for Uncle Sam surface and they are damn near choking me with how thick they are in my throat.

"I…I… can't, Grant. I don't—"

"Don't what?" I step in and take the bag of toiletries from her and toss them on the bed. "Talk to me," I say softly, running my hands down her arms and slipping her hands into mine.

"I don't know how?" Sadness washes over her face and I hear the tears in her voice.

Fuck that. I refuse to let her be scared. That's not the Mercy I know right now and seeing her be so unsure pisses me off. "Sure you do. It's me, sweetheart. Nothing's changed."

I ease onto the bed and pull her into my arms until she's sitting snuggly on my lap. "Why the tears?"

"I missed you, too."

Holding her for the first time after years of dreaming about having her this close has me wondering why the hell we let her have so much space. I have zero intentions of letting another day go by where she's not part of my life. Our lives. She's mentally distanced herself from us and that is all our fault.

She looks so lost. I tighten my arms around her, draw her in and take the first real breath since seeing her when she circles my chest with her arms.

She tucks under my chin and fits so damn nicely in my arms I don't want to let her go ever again.

Gingerly, I pull her back until I can look into those beautiful eyes of hers.

When she raises her chin, her lips part. I try to fight the urge, but I can't help it. I tuck that wayward curl behind her ear, tilt her chin a notch higher and lower my lips to hers.

She closes her eyes, those pretty cheeks flushing, and I take the kiss deeper.

Possessiveness roars through me, and my blood lights on fire. My balls tighten, and my cock swells under her ass. She feels it. I know because she gasps in my mouth, and I stroke my tongue over hers, lavish her with the force of me need, memorizing the confines of that hot little mouth all over again. I'm hot, hard, and ready to take her, but she's not mine alone and I know now is not the time.

"I've imagined turning back the time and erasing that night so many times," she whispers against my lips. She leans in and presses her forehead against mine, and we sit there for a minute. Just breathing each other in.

"Me too," I grunt. I pull her back to look into her eyes. "But only to change my decision to walk away. As inappropriate as that sounds, I wished we would have spread you out right there on the kitchen counter and claimed what we'd been wanting for years."

Her expression turns twenty shades of emotions I have a hard time keeping up with until she lands on the last one I thought what I said would stir.

Anger.

Okay. But damn if she doesn't look hot as hell. My cock pulses.

"You don't get to say that," she demands, jumping up from my lap.

I don't let her get far. I stalk closer and pin her to the wall, both my arms blocking her on either side. Our girl likes to run from the truth and that shit is over. "Why?" I demand.

"Because I've spent the last seven years trying to forget you and the pain your rejection caused and here you are telling me you wished you would have taken me up on my wishes? HA! You don't get a get out of jail free card."

"Who said I am? You think this has been easy on me? On us? Do you think this was just fun and games? Not coming to you, dragging your ass home with us the second you hit eighteen was and still is the hardest fucking thing we've ever lived through?"

"Then why did you? Why did you wait seven damn years, Grant?"

My voice takes on a hard edge that has her flinching but I don't back down. She needs to hear this. "What would your parents think of us? Your brother? After he kicked our asses he would have walked out of our lives, either taking you with him or doing something far worse. You think we wanted that for you? To be the cause of a rift in your family? Your parents don't deserve that, sweetheart."

Her hands are on my chest and her tiny nails are digging into my skin. Good. Let her get all her anger out. I can take it.

Her shoulders are heaving with how hard she is breathing. She looks away. Call me weak but I can't take her not looking at me, so I take her chin in hand and pull her back.

"Tomorrow." She swallows hard as if the words are hard to get out.

I have a feeling I know what's coming next, but I want to force her to say it. "Tomorrow what, baby?" Without trying, she's beautiful. I run a finger over her cheek.

"I want you gone by tomorrow. All of you."

She puts those pretty little hands of hers back on my chest and pushes me out of the room, and I go willingly. For now.

Standing in the doorway, I lean in until our noses are touching. "I think you know we're not going anywhere. Sleep well, princess. Tomorrow is going to be a big day."

I make her hold my gaze until the door is fully closed.

FOUR

No more running. For her and definitely not for us.

I make my way downstairs to find the guys in the living room, beers in hand. Cain holds a cold one up to me as I sink into an armchair closest to the window. Rains have died down to a light drizzle, but you can still see the lightning over the water.

Linc is in a chair on the other side of the room facing the low embers of the fire.

"She okay?"

I scoff. "You heard. This house is like one big echo."

"And?"

"Hell no she's not okay. She's hurting and three brutes just crashed her little solo party, bringing up bad memories for her."

Cain and Linc exchange concerned looks with Cain grumbling something I don't pick up.

"Let's not forget that being a naked solo party," Linc adds, taking a hit off his beer.

Cain leans back and props his beer on his knee. "Anyone else notice how methodical everything was in the kitchen? From the cleaning supplies to how she alphabetized the wine in the fridge. That's not our wild and free-loving life at its fullest Mercy. It's like aliens abducted her and replaced her with a robot or something. Hell, I don't know," he mumbles dragging his hand across the stubble on his chin. "I do know that girl upstairs isn't her."

I shake my head. "You shoulda seen the way her clothes were color-coded upstairs," I say suddenly exhausted just thinking about the amount of work that had to have gone into something like that.

"We left her alone for too damn long. We should have come back sooner."

I had a feeling Cain would bring that up. It's been coming out of his mouth in various forms for the last month.

I glare at him. "You know damn well we couldn't," I counter. "From the way she shoved me out of her room, I'm not too sure we should be here now." That admission sobers me, and I mentally correct my thinking. "But her stubbornness isn't anything new."

With a loud screech that could wake the dead, Linc lugged his chair around to face us both. "No. At least that hasn't changed." He pauses. "No one told you to keep signing up for tour after tour, man; you did that shit on purpose."

I shrug. "And? You were no better. I didn't tell you to follow me."

"You never did, brother. Besides neither of us was about to leave you on your own to get killed."

"I sure the fuck wasn't going to be the one to come home and tell her you were dead." Cain's expression sobers. "It was bad enough we had to come home when Jake died. Thank fuck we didn't have to be the ones to carry that news home."

"It tore me up to leave her the way we did. After the funeral, I mean."

Cain and I both turn to give Linc a look.

I grunt. "It tore us all up, man. But do I need to say it again? We're here now. We have some things to correct and make right. Jake, none of us know how he'd react to this, but we have to believe he'd like to know his sister is loved and cared for."

We all three clink beers.

"So now what? Are we really ready for this? She's not exactly happy we're here."

"We let her sleep tonight and then tomorrow we show her the truth. Telling her we missed her isn't going to be good enough. I just tried that. She's too closed off to her emotions to believe a word we say."

"Now that we have her, we can't let her get away. I'll personally tie her to the bed until she believes us." Cain sucks down the last of his beer and heads to the kitchen for another, leaving his words to hang over us.

I chuckle darkly. "Keep telling yourself that, buddy. For some reason I don't think she'll *let* you do anything."

The light to her room goes dark, and I realize there are only two other beds and one of us will have to take the floor or the lumpy sofa.

Tonight.

Because tomorrow night no one will be sleeping.

FIVE
MERCY

A loud thumping shakes me from my fitful rest. I think I managed a couple of hours, but even that seems generous.

I push myself up in bed, the covers piling around my waist. No sense in denying or wishing last night away. If wishes really worked I'd be living a whole other life.

It's barely daybreak and the birds are out in full swing chirping like the world is a beautiful place. Even the sun is making its appearance over the mountain peaks outside my window. But the pink and purple hues washed over the sky don't make me smile the way they used to.

Thump.

I toss the covers to the side and cross to the lake-facing window. Two stories below I find a brown-haired lumberjack of a man splitting wood in my front yard without a shirt.

Bulging biceps and a back so ripped I can see the muscles bunch and flex with each movement.

FIVE

Grant Cross.

I don't know how but the man had to sense my eyes on him. He turns, flashing me a grin before turning back to chopping wood. He must have been at it for a while with the stack piling up beside him.

I roll my eyes. That man. He pushes all the right—and wrong—buttons.

Cain joins Grant saying something that has them both turning to look up to my window. He pushes buttons too, but a different set. Ones that have me wondering about things I shouldn't like little green-eyed black-haired babies.

I stand there shocked for a moment and try to stay pissed, but it's hard when they grin like that at me. Like their hearts are on their damn sleeves.

I smile back despite the warring feelings inside me. And that was part of the problem. Each of them knew my one weakness. Them.

I step back from the window and head for the shower, giving my closed laptop a long side-eye. Maybe tomorrow...

Frustration fuels a fast wash and rise. When I'm done I slip on a skirt and white tank, wondering if it will draw their attention. Hell, I'd be lying if I said I didn't like it when they eyed my breasts last night.

Before leaving the bedroom I take a moment to twist my hair into a braid, and that's when I see I'm wearing damn near the same outfit from the last time we were all here; I yank off the skirt and toss it aside for a pair of denim shorts instead.

My phone chimes with the arrival of an email.

Oh damn. It's my agent. I've been dreading another email from her.

This won't be good. I don't need to open it to know, but I do anyway.

Holding my breath, I read:

"*Need to hear back from you. It's been three months. This doesn't make us look good.*"

Damn. I know she's right but I still don't have the answer she's looking for. But I need to find one quick. It won't be long before she starts calling and then I'll have to answer.

I close the email app. I can only handle one problem at a time and I currently have three taking over my planned *me* time. And shouldering in like a bunch of brutes.

I leave my phone on the dresser.

I can't hide out up here any longer, I guess. Time to face reality.

I follow the decadent smell of dark vanilla roast and bacon to the kitchen.

I make it down the stairs to find Linc with his back to me, absorbed in his breakfast duties.

Fresh white curtains hang over the bay-styled windows looking out over the lake. Coffee is brewing in a coffeemaker that wasn't there yesterday. Off to the right, I spy a toaster with what smells like bagels and in front of him, Linc is working up a few more strips of bacon and eggs, and on the counter are four plates and matching glasses.

Huh.

Since when did they become the homey type? Whether I liked it or not, the place looks nice and welcoming.

Watching him move gracefully through my kitchen makes my nipples harden behind the soft material of my bra and tank top. I know I should have better control over my body but… uhh…I can't seem to help it.

Worse, my body doesn't want to stop there. I'm flushed and my pussy clenches with excitement, craving one hundred percent of his attention as he turns, beaming at me.

"I guess you drew the short straw?" I say and push deeper into the kitchen. His sweatpants are slung low over his hips with not a stitch of anything else to block the beautiful sight of all that muscle. And the sexy dusting of hair.

I sink onto a barstool and lean on my elbows. His eyes track my movements.

"Morning, sweetheart." He walks around the counter and wraps me in a hug, holding me tight like I'm his and we do this sort of thing every morning. His lips feel wonderful against my cheek one second and then he's gone. Back to his duties.

He reaches over and pours a fresh mug of coffee for me, giving me another shot of his fine ass in those nicely faded sweats I know must be super soft.

Seven years has added a few creases along his brow and the corners of his eyes that have him looking wiser and more handsome. He's tall. Taller than me, but that's not saying much. I only come to just under his chin at five-five. Broad, muscled shoulders, taut pecs and a trim waist, and bulging biceps complete the beautiful package.

I feel the exact thrill of old sensations run through me, knowing how our bodies could feel when pressed together.

Though they are only a few months apart in age, Cain is the only one who looks anything like the younger version of himself. I spy him through the window pulling a lawnmower out of a small shed tucked close to the cabin.

"Still two sugars?" he asks.

"Huh? Oh, yes, please." I turn and take the cup of coffee Linc offers, my fingers brushing over his lightly. "Thanks. You know you don't have to do this. I can cook."

"Why should you when you have three strong men here to take care of you?"

Really? I barely keep my mouth from swinging open. I take my lip between my teeth and raise my mug to my lips. No matter what I do I can't hide the flush that seems to never disappear so I don't try. Since last night's fiasco, I've basically come to the acceptance I'm always going to be red around them.

Mug in hand, I push up from the stool and pretend to ignore what he's said. "You're brave cooking bacon shirtless," I point out. Anything to change the topic.

Typical Linc, he shrugs like it's no different than picking flowers. Leaning a hip on the counter, I snag a few pieces of bacon from the plate and let my eyes slide closed for just a moment. Can't be mad at a man cooking your bacon.

"It's all about precision."

My eyes dart to his.

He holds up a lid to shield the popping grease and wields a black spatula as some makeshift sword.

I can't help but laugh. But on the flip side, seeing him like this, playing house like everything is hunky-dory, just makes my heart ache for times lost.

Damn it.

I draw back. I'll enjoy my coffee, eat the bacon and then after that be on my way since they refuse to budge.

I take my cup of coffee and stroll out to the deck to see Cain with his shirt tucked into his back pocket, ball cap turned around and sweat running over fine rippling muscles as he fights back the weeds that have overtaken the front yard, the lawnmower left off to the side.

I guess I really wasn't dreaming last night.

The creak of the spring on the screen door sounds, and in the next second Lincoln is standing behind me, smoothing his arm around my waist.

I turn my head and look up at him. "What are you doing?" I ask, placing my empty hand over his.

Instead of answering, he holds out a toasted bagel with peach jam and passes it under my nose.

"Peace offering?"

"Oh no," I groan, knowing my resolve is about to cave. "That's not fair." My brows pinch. "Mom's jam?" I swivel my head, locking eyes with him. "I guess that's where you got the curtains and coffeemaker?" I ask, already knowing the obvious.

He pulls my ass flush against him, causing me to shiver. Let me tell you, old worn sweats do nothing to hide a man's hard cock and he feels like steel pressed into the crease of my ass. Shorts or no shorts, there's no missing the promise he's saying without the use of words.

I knew my momma was up to something, and I guess that something was sending these three to me. I can't help but wonder if she knows what that means. Or if what I'm thinking would disappoint her in any way. My poppa too.

This is wrong. God help me. I know wanting three men is wrong in so many ways. Inappropriate and socially unacceptable. I couldn't help it back then, and I sure the hell haven't learned how to in the time since.

"Linc," I whisper, forcing the heat from my body into the soles of my feet.

His hand slides up to slip under my tank and rest flat against my stomach, holding me again like I'm his. He leans in and inhales the scent of my shampoo.

"Strawberries and vanilla. Just like I remember."

His dark eyes plead with me as he waves the jam-covered breakfast under my nose, and I know it won't take much more to make me cave. It's not the food I want, but the man.

I feel the other men's eyes on me, and I turn away from Linc to look out from the porch. Grant, ax in hand, has a look of hope and Cain, damn it, he does too.

I raise my eyes to Linc's, searching for some kind of sign he wouldn't push me away. After all this time of wishing for exactly what he's doing, my heart says to trust my gut, but my head wonders what he is playing at. There has to be some game here.

The sweet scent of peaches has my mouth watering and I can't hold on anymore. I balance the mug of coffee on the porch railing and take the bagel, sinking my teeth in with a loud groan. "How did you remember?" I ask around a mouthful of Heaven.

He strokes the rough pad of his thumb over my lip, and I look on hungrily as he puts it between his lips, sucking off the peach jam.

Fuuuuck. That was hot.

"I remember every single detail about you," he says with a small smile that does a fine job of softening me up. "You can ask me anything from the day I met you till now and I'd be able to recall. I even remember what you looked like in your bathing suit when you tried out for the high school swim team. The boys do too." He nods to his friends.

He nuzzles my neck.

"Hmm…I looked cute," I recall, taking another bite and doing a crappy job ignoring how good his lips on my skin feel.

"That red number didn't quite fit, the way I remember, and that's what we loved the most. Didn't quite fit those beautiful tits and plump, juicy ass. You had every dick in school hard for six solid months including the dirty-ass teachers. They looked but we made sure none of them tried to touch."

That was news to me. Hmm. Come to think of it, maybe that's why Mr. Fox, my twelfth-grade biology professor kept dogging me all year.

I smirk, knowing what I'm about to say will hit a few buttons. "Did I? There was this one teacher I liked." I let out a faux sigh. "But yeah, I never really noticed anyone else, besides him." Emphasis on *him*.

But I did.

Boy did I ever.

I remember watching Lincoln jack off in his room after spending an afternoon with us down by the lake. We'd played, enjoyed a great barbecue, and after the sunset he'd carried me back to my room when I fell asleep using his lap as my pillow.

He thought I was asleep, but when I heard heavy grunts coming from down the hall, I was curious.

He didn't know I watched him fist his cock through the glass shower door and work his length until white-hot liquid spilled all over his fist. When my name fell from his lips I knew what I had to do.

Or at least I thought I did.

That night I nearly screamed my own release from the bathroom door, but I managed to run back to my room on shaky legs. I pleasured myself three times that night.

Linc mutters a curse under his breath, and I hide my smile behind another bite of bagel.

"And I remember more," Linc whispers close to my ear.

I arch a brow and take another bite, knowing all my secrets. "That's kinda scary."

Linc's chest rumbles with a masculine laugh. "Is it? You'll have to try me out sometime. We can play a game of strip truth and dare. You never know what I might share."

Hmmm, the younger me would jump all over that. Three turns and I could have him stripped naked. Grant and Cain too.

Speaking of, from the corner of my eye I see them finish their tasks and head for the hose coiled at the end of the porch. The front yard is weeded and ready for the grass to be cut, leaving only the lonely flowerbeds in need of loving.

But those can wait.

Seconds is all it takes in the early morning heat and they are standing naked in my yard. I crunch into my bagel in Linc's arms, watching his best friend strip out of a dirty pair of jeans to reveal…

Hells fire.

Lincoln's lips are on my neck, tasting, teasing. "See something you like, baby?"

He knows damn well I do.

But a heated "huh-uh," is about all I manage. I'm too busy taking in all the glorious six feet four inches of solid muscle to put any real thought into my words. And make that all times two, because Cain is hosing down right alongside Grant.

They're so close water splashes off them to wet me.

Steady rivulets of water run over all that tanned skin, and I'm suddenly parched. My heart is thumping so loud there's no way Linc isn't hearing it.

He traces the tip of his tongue over my pulse point.

Fuck.

I shudder my eyelids.

The hiss of my zipper sliding down has both of us groaning. My pulse jackhammers and I suck in air between my teeth when he slides under the band of my panties and he pushes deeper, finding my slit dripping wet.

"Linc," I moan, not sure what else to say. It's all too much, too fast. Too damn good.

My arousal soaks his palm and my panties. My soft pussy lips part for him with the slightest pressure, and I spread my thighs as he sinks a finger in.

"Ah, fuck, you're hot and tight."

I grind my hips and press the palm of his hand against my clit, rubbing the nub and riding his finger.

As Linc slowly finger fucks me, I look on as Cain and Grant run their hands over their sculpted abs and further until they have their strong hands wrapped around and stroking their heavy cocks in the late morning light.

God save me. I can't breathe.

Sun glints off all those angles and God bless the military for making the boys I knew the men I'm seeing today.

Water slides and splashes over them, and right now I wonder what it would be like to pool over them like that, touch every contour and lick every delicious inch of them.

Linc growls, a low sound that just barely hits my ears but has me shivering all the same.

"I like that naughty look in your eye, baby. That's it, just like that. Make my hand all wet and sticky." He tips my chin up and leans in until I'm pinned against the railing. "I hope you slept well, baby. Today is going to be a long day for you."

What does that mean?

All the feelings I had for him come rushing back the second all that muscle molds to all of my dips and curves, which are noticeably curvier than the last time he held me like this. From the hard dick pressing into my ass, I'd say he notices too and his hard cock apparently appreciates.

Linc dips a second finger in, stretching my virgin hole and my knees start shaking, but he holds me up, coffee and bagel long forgotten on the railing.

He strokes in and out of my velvety walls and then as I watch pulls his fingers free and slides them between his lips, sucking them clean.

Breathing hard and finally free of his touch I push out of his arms. This is all too much. "Wait," I tell him when he holds a hand out for me. Cain and Grant come up behind me on the stairs like a wall of muscle and I push past them, buttoning my shorts.

"Just wait a minute. This is all too fast. I haven't seen you guys in seven years and you think we can just pick back up where we left off?"

"In a way. That night you were firmly off-limits. Now you're not."

"Cain!" I plant my hands on my hips.

"You ask, expect to get the truth back. That's how this is going to work."

I hold up a finger like it's going to keep the three wolves in their place. "Truth, okay…okay, you want the truth? Since I have all three of you together let me get real for a second."

I pull my hair off my neck and into a ponytail. It's more than the growing summer heat working me into a sweat right now.

"When you boys finish, you know where your cars are parked. I expect you to be gone before I get back from my hike or I'll call the sheriff and report trespassing, and you can tell Mom you did what she asked on your long drive back to the city. There. Job done. *Hasta luego.*" I smile, giving my brother's best friends a mocking salute.

I don't need them or anyone. I've been fine alone all this time and I'll continue to be that way.

I make to turn around and head back to my room until they get the message I'm not interested, but Grant's words pull me right back around.

"You're scared because you feel something. Linc made you realize you wanted something with all your heart and then you freaked out, realizing you could actually have it. You just have to stop running long enough to grab it."

"You think you can read minds now?"

Grant, in all his naked glory, crosses his arms over his chest. "No, I just know *you*."

Screw this. What the hell do they know? They haven't lost half of what I have. I bet they don't even realize what they did to my young heart by giving me their backs when they walked away. Before the tears have a chance to come, I turn on my heel and aim for my car, but Linc is off the porch and across the yard before I make it. I yelp when I'm pulled off my feet and slung over a broad shoulder.

"Lincoln Masters, put me down, you big brute. You can't do this to me!" I slap at his back, but he doesn't flinch. In fact, he laughs and damn if Cain and Grant don't have the wickedest fucking smiles on their faces.

"Sorry, little girl, you're not going anywhere until we say."

SIX
LINCOLN

"You're not going anywhere; we're not going anywhere. NONE of us are going anywhere." I haul a very pissed-off Mercy over my shoulder and clamp one arm over her legs and another over her delightfully stubborn ass. I can still taste her juices on my tongue, and that is what makes this easier to do. I know she wants us. Or her young, tight cunt wouldn't be dripping wet for us.

"Scream at me all you want," I offer. "We're not leaving this cabin until we have a little—or long—chat. Whatever it takes. Now stop wiggling your hot little body or you might make us do something about that wet pussy of yours right here on the front lawn for everyone passing by on their fancy boats. And all before we've planned it, too."

A naked Cain and Grant fall in beside me like escorts as I cross the yard in half the time it took Mercy on her shorter legs. Damn our girl can move when she wants to, though.

"Planned?"

"Yep. I don't fancy grass stains on my ass but if that's what it takes, okay by us."

Grant and Cain sound off beside me in agreement.

Her feminine hands are on my back, pounding, but she doesn't realize I'll take her hands on me anyway I can get them.

"Put me down you, big bear."

"Nope."

I chuckle when she growls her frustration.

A few more strides and I'm up the stairs doing as the little princess demands, setting her down.

The second I step back she cocks a hip and props her hand on it like that's going to get any of us to move out of her way any time soon. "What do you mean planned?" she spits. "Don't play games with me. I got the message loud and clear last time. If you don't recall let me tell you word for word in case your brains have stopped working… in the words of your friend over there," she shoots daggers at Grant who only crosses his arms over his chest with no issues being naked while we get down to business with our girl.

She takes a finger and pokes each of us in the chest. "In no way did I misunderstand the 'no, not gonna happen. Our dicks won't be getting anywhere near that fuckable pussy. Forget it.' And I know I didn't hallucinate you three walking away from me. You only came back for my brother's funeral five years later and *then* you were off again."

"We did come back. Who do you think has kept this place from going to the weeds and squatters, woman? The only reason it's overgrown now is because we were away on duty."

SIX

She's seething, but I understand her anger and hurt. It seems the other men do too.

Cain's rough voice has her mouth hanging open a bit and her words drying up. "We were here. It was you who didn't bother."

Grant's eyes narrow on her. "And what I said was taken out of context, young lady." Grant, being Grant, doesn't give any room for argument. He really needs to learn how to give a little in order to get something in return.

He always was the hardheaded one of us all.

But, that got her going all the same. And, I can't deny the madder we can get her the faster her true feelings will boil to the surface. When that happens, we can deal with everything once and for all and help her. But not all her wrath and ire can be blamed on us.

"Young lady? I'm not the young, hormonal girl who looked at you with infatuation anymore, Grant. I've grown up and, in the process, I've realized a lot about myself."

"We know you're not, Mercy baby, and that's why all the kid gloves are off and you're going to get everything you asked for. If you let us. You just have to open up and let us in."

"Who says that's what I want?"

Cain cracks a smirk that turns into a roguish smile if I ever saw one. "You're still here talking to us, aren't you?" The sweet-talking SOB has her hand in his and her eyes trailing over his hard cock. I feel a stab of jealousy when the tight lines around her eyes soften for him.

Not jealousy for my friend but of her easy affections. He always did know how to get to her when Grant and I hit her walls. Stubborn minx. Always has been, but with Cain, we at least had an in. And we were about to use it for the benefit of all four of us.

She looks between each of us surrounding her on all sides. But she keeps the steel in her backbone and I don't know any other woman who can stand up and hold her ground against three alphas. But our Mercy does.

"Things have changed," she all but whispers. "All I want is to be left alone. I came up here for one reason and as soon as that is done, I'm gone. I don't need you. Any of you. You hurt me once, so have others, and I'm done. I'm done with all the rejection."

I cross my arms and rock back on my heels. My hard dick tents my pants, and she notices in a big way. Whether she realizes it or not, the way she's biting her bottom lip tells us everything her words don't. "Liar," I say. "Remember you're getting the truth from now on and I'm straight up calling your bluff."

"We all are," Grant adds beside me, in a gruff voice.

For a second she does nothing but work her mouth in what seems to be a moment of complete shock at what she hears.

Good. Shock I can work with. It's the walls that give me trouble.

I nod once at Grant, and he swings the porch door open. I shuffle her inside, not letting the little she-devil get by us. No more running for any of us.

Cain hits the power button on the air conditioner, and in seconds a cool blast kills the summer heat.

She looks on as we surround her in the middle of the living room. Cain to her left with Grant on her right, and I'm right where I want to be standing behind her as she turns in a circle.

I wrap my arms around her middle, and she doesn't fight me, so that's some ground we've won.

I lean in. "Tell you what. How about for every lie you give us we give you a nice spanking on that tight little ass of yours. I've counted at least five." I tick off each of them.

"You thinking you're not running, you thinking you don't need anyone, trying to convince us *we* don't want *you*." I tsk. "Naughty girl. How'm I doing so far?"

Her eyes dart between all of us and she swallows thickly, crossing her arms over her chest, pushing her ripe tits high. I don't mind. Those dark nipples of hers are jutted out and pressing against her tank, teasing us with the truth.

"Don't forget how she wants to be left all alone up here in the middle of nowhere, but that sweet pussy is wetter than a garden hose for us," Cain adds as a matter-of-fact to a blushing Mercy.

"Ah yes, and how she wishes she could erase our first kiss."

"Oh damn, baby, that hurts." I hold a hand over my heart for the full effect.

Looking at her, Cain pulls out all the stops. "Sounds fair. I'd love to see all that beautiful flesh again and turn it a rosy pink under our touch. I've been hard since seeing those pretty pink folds and ass thrust in the air last night." I flash Cain a side grin and watch as he rubs his hands together.

"You wouldn't." she dares us in a breathy tone.

I tip her chin up until she's looking into my eyes, and I draw in her sweet scent of strawberries and vanilla. "We most definitely would and will. That pretty flash of pink over your skin tells us you just might like what we're promising if you keep lying to us and most importantly, to yourself."

Grant steps close enough to where, with a twitch of her hand, Mercy could reach out and wrap her feminine hand around his dick. "The truth is you came up here to continue hiding away instead of being back in the city with your parents giving them the love they deserve. The comfort of knowing you are safe. You've been traveling all over the world, never staying in one spot long enough to make connections and dodging coming home after Jake died. Before that even."

"Is he telling the truth?" I ask, softly, brushing the backs of my knuckles over her cheek. "Talk to us, baby." I take one of her small hands in mine and lift it to my lips, pressing a kiss to her open palm.

"Let us in. Please, Mercy. We only want to help." Cain kneels in front of her, anchoring her to us by placing his hands on her hips. He runs the tip of his tongue over the flash of tanned skin just below her tank top, and she quivers in my arms.

"How…how is it you all know this about me?"

"Fuck, Mercy, you're killing us. Please don't cry, honey." I wipe at a tear.

She looks up, her eyes finally open and really seeing us standing in front of her.

I pull her over to the sofa and hold a hand out for her to sit on my lap. I don't realize I'm holding my breath until she takes my hand and glides that sweet ass over my lap. For a second I worried she would refuse.

Grant kneels in front of her, and Cain comes to sit beside me, moving her legs into his lap.

He fingers that wayward curl always slipping from any form of restraint and tucks it behind her ear. "You thought we didn't care what happened to Jake's little sister? To the girl that always greeted us with open arms and warm kisses every time we came home? Damn, girl, you're the reason we made it through some hellish close calls in the first place."

Grant leans over Mercy and grabs his wallet off the side table and pulls a worn piece of what looks like paper out, but it's way more than that to the three of us.

He holds up a small four-by-three picture, creased from folding and unfolding, of her sitting on my lap, arms around my neck, Grant and Cain on either side. The world shone in her eyes that night.

We were out front next to the lake sitting around a huge bonfire, our sweet girl, us and Jake. I don't remember what we were celebrating or if we were just hanging out like we did so many times. We'd already graduated high school and had a couple of years under our belt in college while on Uncle Sam's payroll. Shit, come to think about it. I think that might have been the best day of my life up until now.

She pales a little in my arms, and I help her sit up a bit. She gingerly takes the photo and sees what we've known way before it was remotely acceptable—a whole lot more than just friendship in her eyes as she gazes over at Grant. We've all seen the same look in her eyes every time she looks at any of us. Only this time we caught it with a picture.

In the candid shot my arms are around her much like they are now and I'm leaning toward Cain saying something, and she's sneaking a look at Grant with so much love it's damn near tangible even all these years later.

She's silent for a moment, and I can tell her anger has died and so has the sadness.

I take that back. I see a sadness in her eyes I hate to admit may never go away. But I see happiness there too. Maybe I'm seeing things, but I sure the hell hope I'm not. Selfish as that sounds.

"Who took this?" she whispers quietly. She runs her delicate fingers over our faces and then the younger version of herself. Probably thinking the same thing I am. Wishing she could turn back the time and do things differently.

Something tight and sharp in my chest lessens its hold when her muscles relax and she lets me hold her a little closer.

"Jake," I answer. "He gave it to Grant the night we left here. He knew the deployment coming up for us would…be hard," I finish, after a pause, not wanting to go into a lot of detail. The shit we've done for flag and country has taken its pound of flesh from each of us in different ways, but she doesn't need to know the horrors we've lived to understand she's the angel that will save our souls. From the looks on their faces, I'm pretty damn sure my buddies feel the same way I do right now—relieved she's not fighting us anymore.

"We each made a copy and carry it everywhere we go." Cain runs his hands up her leg and she reaches for him.

Seeing my buddy mold his lips around her knuckles and the smile it stirs from her has my dick getting hard. The only thing we've ever wanted is for Mercy to be happy.

"When I thought things were bad and I might not make it back, this picture gave me the strength to come home." Grant taps the edge of the picture and her tiny fingers are shaking like a leaf.

"Me too," I add.

"All of us," Cain corrects. "All of us needed you."

Grant wraps her fingers around the picture. "It brought us home. Now I want you to have it. To know you're home too, and this is why you need to stay." He taps the picture.

"Home," she repeats like it's some foreign word to her.

Grant leans over her. "Home. Right here with us. We've tracked you from Peru to Australia to Germany and Canada." He takes her chin in hand. "I hope you got it out of your system, Mercy because you're done running, sweetheart."

"Really?" She sounds distinctly cocky all of a sudden, and I smirk, loving the defiance in our girl. She's a fighter if nothing else. But she still doesn't believe us. She wants to but her walls are built out of anger and that shit is tougher than a ton of cement. It's going to take more than talking to break through it. Grant locks eyes with me over her head, and I know he's thinking the same.

"Why are you telling me all this? It's all too late. Nice to know, but too late." She pauses and it seems she's struggling with the way she's tugging her bottom lip between her teeth. "I have a flight in a couple of hours, and I need to get ready."

She actually believes herself.

She takes a shaky breath.

"Since you have a hard time hearing, I think we need to go another route." Cain takes her leg in hand and trails kisses up her thigh, stopping at the hem of her shorts. He moves between her legs, and we all catch the hitch in her breath and the moan on her lips.

"Open for him, baby," I command softly when she turns her eyes up to mine. And I know she understands what I'm asking for is more than just her legs.

Grant chimes in. "I agree. I think it's time to show our baby girl the truth." He leans forward, a hunger in his eyes. "Do you know what happened the last time you wore something this short around us?" I look on as my friend's expression turns dark and hungry.

"Not really." But I see her gaze dip to Cain's hard-on and then Grant's.

My balls draw up tight, and I want nothing more than to see those sassy lips wrap around my cock.

My chuckle is dry for lack of humor. "Liar. I know you remember making yourself squirt all those sweet juices all over your thighs for us. So now that makes six spankings you've earned."

"That time was wholly inappropriate, but you're not jailbait anymore and this time, Mercy baby, we get to lick all that juicy girl cum off your tender body. But not before a good and thorough spanking on that plump ass of yours." Cain's eyes hold a glint of satisfaction that has my cock pulsing, and I know she feels it.

Her jaw drops. "You can say what you want. I don't have time for any more of your rejections or anyone else's for that matter." Her growled retort is delivered like a slap across the face. She tries to wiggle off my lap, and I clamp a hand over her thighs.

"You're not running this time, baby. We told you. It's time for you to face the music."

"Linc," she begs. Her breathing becomes heavy and her lips part.

SIX

"Remember when I told you after Jake's funeral that we would always take care of you?"

She nods. "Yeah."

I see a glimmer of something in her eyes, and I know what that something is. It's curiosity and hunger.

"You have to let us make good on that promise, baby, and we'll take as much of the pain away as earthly possible." I run a finger over her shoulder, and the strap of her tank slips. I lean in and press my lips to her soft, supple skin.

Her brows lift a fraction in surprise, but there's a shift in her expression. One that rivals Grant's but it's gone before I can make a move on the lust I see in those baby blues. The truth is clear as the skies outside. She likes what we're saying, but she's still trying to deny herself any sort of happiness.

But before anything, something nags at me.

"What rejection?" I ask darkly, with a warning look. "Who rejected you, baby? Who could ever say no to you? You're fucking temptation on two beautiful legs."

Anger that she would let anyone but us touch her flares up but then again, we stayed away and in doing that gave up all claim to her. But there's jealousy if I'm honest. I'm only human. But she's ours now and that's all that matters.

I watch her face go blank, and then a fiery hell flashes in her eyes and has her looking madder than the Devil in winter. "Just about every damn man in my life starting with you three."

Well fuck. I lean back into the sofa. "You want to keep pushing on that? Okay. Time for that spanking, boys." And I mean every damn word.

SEVEN
MERCY

He means every word. I know he does. I recognize the grit and determination that comes over him when he sets his mind to doing something. I just never had it all squarely focused on me before now, and it makes me squirm.

Admittedly, I like it. My body doesn't do such a good job of hiding the truth either. The silk strip of my panties is soaked and I can feel it getting wetter by the second.

Still, a fierce blush flashes across my cheeks at the dirty image of all three men seeing, touching and spanking my ass.

I close my eyes, taking a steadying breath.

What is wrong with me? I want to bury my face in my hands, but I hold back just barely. The only thing more embarrassing than getting wet at their promised punishment is letting them know it.

I didn't mean to throw the past at them or to hurt any of them, that's just not who I am, but I see the pain I've caused stare back at me from the men I once loved.

"What does that mean? You're not really going to spank me." Playing coy really isn't me either, but I'm trying to buy myself some time to mentally prepare.

Linc narrows his dark eyes, but it's Cain who answers. "Exactly what he said, Mercy baby. Remember you're getting only the truth from us."

"We've always loved you, but evidently our word isn't good enough," Grant grumbled lowly. "Let's show it. I want to see that ass rosy pink from our hands. One for every lie you want to keep between us. That damn wall of yours is going to come down one way or another."

"Wall?" I ask. But I know what he's talking about. The first cement block went up the second the three of them turned their backs on me and each day a new one went up, held in place by all the anger I've felt toward them.

God, that makes me sound so bitter, but in reality, I'm just tired of being hurt all the time. No man has ever touched me the way they have, and it's stolen any chances of me ever being intimate with anyone. I've tried, but much to my disappointment and others, I've never gotten past second base. It's been close. But the second anything close to sex happens I close up.

All because it was never them touching me.

But I refuse to let them know that.

I hear the sincerity in Grant's words, but I can't bring myself to believe they know what love means. It means you do anything it takes to be with the ones you love. Not running off to war. How when they left me to believe the opposite for so long? That plays with a woman's mind. To flip a switch? Nah. Not that easy.

Or maybe it is? I think I'm about to find out.

I blink back at Lincoln, and I can see he's no longer playing.

I swallow thickly.

A spanking.

I roll the word around in my mind, and I'm not sure what turns me on more. The flash of dark hunger in Cain's eyes. Grant's humorless chuckle, or the way Lincoln's hand clamps down on my thighs.

"I don't need any man's hands on my ass." Okay, that wasn't even believable to my ears, but I wasn't about to just *let* them.

"Is that so?" Lincoln's powerful tone makes my body drip with hot liquid. I can feel it soak through my panties to wet my shorts.

"I need to leave," I say, but I can't seem to make myself pull from their arms and make good on my words.

Linc's energy swarms around me, and Cain and Grant aren't any different. Every inhale takes me deeper under their spell. All three carry a forceful power, it fills every room they enter, and right now it's wrapping me up in their energy and not letting me think.

Grant grabs me tight around the waist, and Linc buries a hand in my hair, turning me toward him.

His claiming lips are on mine and his tongue diving in the second Cain frees the button and zipper of my shorts. I gasp into Lincoln's hot mouth, and he eats it up like candy, giving me a throaty groan. His fingers curl deeper into my hair, pulling me closer.

He eases back, looking like he wants to devour me, and those dark brown eyes of his are so captivating I find it nearly impossible to pull away.

"Now kiss Grant like that," Linc rasps, his lips brushing over mine. "I want to watch him fuck your mouth with his tongue."

My chest is heaving, and my heart is pounding. I turn to find my blue-eyed lover eating me up with his gaze. Stroking the length of soft jawline with the tip of his finger, he holds me captive as sensations overwhelm me. His hands replace Linc's in my hair, turning me toward him.

My lips part for Linc's best friend. I'm playing with fire, letting my desires take over when my heart is screaming for me to steal back my willpower. To leave and never come back.

I hollow my cheeks and suck Grant's tongue. He growls into my mouth, and I eat that up too.

His kiss is more dominant than Linc's and Cain's.

Commanding and powerful. Hungry.

Like I'm his last meal and he's going to enjoy every bite and drop of juice I have to offer. Using his other hand, the tips of his fingers whisper over my exposed nipples, forcing a groan from me, driving me crazy wild for what they do next.

Grant pulls back with a wicked grin, his lips wet from our shared kiss. "Are you ready?"

I'm torn. Yes, I want to feel. No, I don't want the residual emotions that come with it.

But my only answer is a yelp when Cain has my shorts and panties off with one pull, exposing my bare pink folds to them with Cain pinning my legs open.

My whole body burns for these three gorgeous, large men.

Grant flips me over and spreads me out over Linc's lap. His muscled legs support me, and I have my ass in the air. Heat pools between my legs and slicks my velvety-soft folds. I squirm but Linc clamps an arm over my hips, pinning me in place.

"How does that pussy look, Cain," Grant asks, locking starving eyes with me.

I turn to look over my shoulder to see Cain come up to his knees behind me, and before I can gasp or squirm, his hands are spreading my ass cheeks wide for all of them to look at me.

"Like a peach. I told you. Didn't I? I said our girl would be ripe and ready for us. Look at all that cream. Hold her open, boys. I want to taste the before and then the after."

Oh my God.

I thought I could not blush any redder. But I can and do when Lincoln sinks his strong fingers into my ass cheek and Grant follows on the other. Both squeeze, exposing me with a light pull.

Grant is kneeling by my head and I can't help but lick my lips at seeing the drop of cum slip from the tip of his dick when I swivel to look his way.

The heavy girth hangs between his legs, his balls full of milk for me. Now I'm really torn. Because I want to know what it's like to take all three, feel their cum on my body and take me bare.

Grant catches me looking. "Bad girls don't get to taste before their punishment."

I drag my eyes off his hard dick and up his chest, but the quip on the end of my tongue about bad girls being the best is lost.

SEVEN

Cain makes sure of it. He's between my legs, dragging his hot, wet tongue from my aching clit to my dripping hole.

His teasing thumb rims my most intimate part, making me squirm and gasp. "What are you doing? Oh, fuck." I hang my head, breathing heavily.

Grant's hand slides down my back and over the swell of my ass.

I arch into his touch and groan a tiny sound.

"You're done running, Mercy. I told you that already, but it's time you realized we're not playing."

"We're not like your young college boyfriends. You want to see what happens when you wear tiny shorts and tease three grown fucking men suffering from seven years' worth of blue balls?" At some point my ponytail has slipped out and my hair falls over part of my face and shoulder. Linc reaches out and brushes it to the side so he can look me in the eye.

"Answer him, sweetheart."

I'm not stupid or naïve so much to think this is anything other than them wanting to exert their dominance over me. I'm game. I can play. But like hell I'm dropping my guard just because they tell me to.

A hand on each cheek, a sudden burst of hot air hits my drenched slit, and I nearly cum right there. It is insane to think I can orgasm from so little, but I've wanted them so bad and my body has been dreaming of this for so long. Not to mention, it's Cain and that man could walk by me and my pussy would squirt.

Honestly, maybe I should let go a little. Let them work my body, get them out of my system and *then* walk away.

That sounds ridiculous even to me. But one thing is true. My silence has provoked them and I'm going to pay for it.

Smack.

A sharp sting registers before the sound of flesh hitting flesh hits my ears.

I gasp.

"What the fuck! Did you just—

"—spank that delicious ass, hell yes. We're not going to stop until you admit the truth."

"Wha—"

My moans are muffled when I drop my head into Linc's lap, trying to concentrate on his words and not the burn blazing through my core. Hell's fire blooms out from the point of contact, and my ass arches into Cain's hand without me realizing it until his strong, rough hand rubs the pain in like a balm on my ass.

I'm panting. Hard. And oddly turned on so fast a sheen of sweat breaks out over me.

I'm in so much trouble, because…oh God help me, because I liked it. A lot.

Through blurry eyes, I look up into Linc's dark gaze.

He hooks a finger under my chin. Something he likes to do a lot, I notice. They all do. It's like their little game of control over me, because once I look into their eyes I'm powerless to pull away. "You're going to tell us the truth and it might sting a little, but I promise you'll love it, too."

I already do.

I bite my lip, my heart pounding. Hot liquid pools between my legs to soak my thighs and pussy. When I feel the pulse of Lincoln's cock under me, I moan. And this time everyone hears me. My nails dig into his leg. "Please," I plead but I don't know if I'm begging for them to stop or them to do it again.

Smack.

Three and four come in quick secessions and I cry out, my back bowing. Grant is bent over me dragging a finger through my soaked cunt and he's back in front of me licking it clean.

"Again," he says. "She's sweet, but not ready for us just yet."

Cain grips my ass, each of his fingers pressing into my flesh making the pain fade into something I never expected. Pleasure. And then he slides his hand down to cup me, spreading me wide. I turn in time to watch him lean in and swipe his tongue over my pussy, making my walls clench and me cry out.

"Sweeter than honey, Mercy baby. Just how I imagined, but Grant's right," he groans, pulling away. I see my juices run down his chin and a satisfied look in his eyes.

"Here, taste."

My pulse beats frantically at what he's asking—no—telling me to do.

"Taste your juices on his fingers, baby. Lick them clean."

My mouth falls open on Linc's command. Fuck.

I turn my gaze up to Grant's as he presses a thumb to my chin for me to open. It's easy to comply and when I do, Cain's wet fingers glide over my tongue. I lick hungrily, making me buck against Linc's hold on me as Cain moves away.

"Easy, baby, we've got you," Linc comforts me, tethering me to earth when I would float away. "Greedy, baby," he murmurs close to my ear. Beneath me his hard cock jerks, and I can feel the wetness of his cum through the material of his sweats.

The next hand comes down on my left cheek this time. Firm skin on skin. I cry out from the mixture of pleasure-pain that shoots through me like bolts of lightning. I'm panting hard, pushing back into whoever is doing the spanking, no longer caring.

"Come on. Open that sweet mouth and tell us what we want to hear."

That's Grant. His big hand is wrapped around his shaft, and he's stroking it in slow movements, making me hungrier. But it's the look in his eyes that has me questioning if I really think they are doing this only to punish me for staying away.

"Or we keep going."

Cain.

Smack.

My ass jiggles under their hands, and my eager pussy clenches.

"Look at all that rosy pink on this beautiful ass. Do I keep going? It's making me hot and harder for a piece of that ass, Mercy baby." Cain presses the length of his hot, bare cock between my cheeks and rubs a hand over the burning, sting. The dirty, raw image of me spread under three men as they claim my body sends pulses of forbidden lust through me.

I turn to lock gazes with my green-eyed torturer. "Wh…what? Tell you what?"

The walls of my pussy clench, and every fiber of my being sizzles.

Smack.

"Arg," I cry out and fall into the pain as it fades into an all-consuming pleasure. My pussy clenches again, this time pulsating with a desperate need for the thick, throbbing cocks it craves.

"The truth. Or we walk."

I peer over my shoulder.

"Fine. I don't really have a flight, and I don't really want you to leave." That's all I could give.

Smack.

"And?"

Damn Lincoln and his know-it-all self.

"And?" Linc's hand soothes over the swell of my ass to slip between my ass cheeks.

I shudder when his thumb strokes over my puckered hole. "Yes. Yes, I'm done running," I pant.

Hells fire, I'm done. I feel in my soul it's the solid truth. I just don't know if I'll be running to them.

"And I'm coming," I shout. Fire hotter than blue flames roar through me as an orgasm hits my core, making my insides convulse with pleasure so heady I can't stop.

"That's it, baby. Squirt that release all over Cain's face," Grant purrs.

I turn to see Cain dipping low, and can't hold back my cry of need when his tongue is on me, licking and sucking. Another release hits, smaller than the last when Cain sucks my pleasure nub between his hot, hungry lips.

All three chuckle. "Good girl," Grant purrs by my ear. "That earns you a reward."

EIGHT
MERCY

Grant...those words...

Mmm, yes! I shudder from what I hope they imply.

Because sex I can do. Love is something entirely different, but you don't have to love someone to enjoy them fucking you. Even if it is my first time.

Right?

It's the other stuff I want no part of. The deep feelings I see in their eyes and the way they touch me.

There's a short silence, and then I'm whirled around and clinging to Grant's neck as he picks me up and carries me over to a pile of thick blankets spread out in front of the dark fireplace. There are several pillows thrown around, making it look like someone slept here last night.

Grant gingerly lays me down, resting my head on a pillow, and I immediately know it was him who slept here last night from the soft scent of his cologne on my pillow.

I hear a groan come from Cain, who is on his knees between my thighs, stroking a hand from the base of his dick to the head, forcing drops of cum from the slit. His eyes are on my throbbing, aching clit, making me whimper to feel his tongue there again.

Linc spreads out beside me. Wet heat soaks his hand when he reaches between my legs and parts my pussy lips for Cain. "Sit up a little on your elbows, baby. I want you to watch him eat your tight little hole."

I do as instructed and wither in surprise when the stubble from Cain's jaw rakes against my tender flesh. Shock and awe shoot through me, and I buck my hips, whimpering.

Linc clamps a hand over my stomach, holding me down.

"Shhh, baby." Firm hands spread my thighs, and my head falls back when Cain's hot wet tongue flicks over the nub between my folds. "Yes," I cry out unable to hold back. Heat blazes through me.

"Our Mercy is a dirty little princess. Look at how wet that cunt is. Sweeter after our spanking."

Linc's massive erection throbs against my bare thigh as he pulls my legs wider for his friend.

To my right Grant pushes to his knees, his leaking cock dripping over my breasts. Pinned between the three of them, I feel like I'm turning into a puddle of goo. I can no longer control my body's reaction to them, not that I ever could, so I fall into the ecstasy of having my wildest fantasies come true.

"Take his cock, baby, and suck him off." Linc turns my head to his friend. Having Linc watch makes me wilder and wetter as I wrap my fingers around the hot length of Grant's cock. Cain seems to like the effect as he slurps up my juices. He's so thick my fingers barely close, and the head of his cock looks angry, undoubtedly in need of some loving.

I part my lips and moan around his thick girth as he sinks in, hitting the back of my throat.

I work him as he slowly pulls out and then feeds me his cock all over again.

The salty-sweet taste of his cum hits my tongue, and I hollow my cheeks, sucking harder, unabashedly craving more.

My pulse jumps, thumping wildly in my chest. Beside me, Linc takes my other hand and wraps his larger one around mine over his dick.

Fuck, this is hot.

I hold Grant's eyes as I jerk Linc off and Cain eats my pussy.

It feels so good all I want to do is close my eyes and revel in all the sensations pounding into me.

"Look at me. Don't you dare close those beautiful blue eyes. I want you to see each of us giving and taking pleasure from each other."

He rocks his hips, driving and pulling his cock from my mouth.

He stills to a stop and slips his shaft from my lips, dips and takes my mouth in a claiming kiss.

"My turn," he says gruffly and I am not left wondering what he's talking about long.

He switches with Cain. I groan around his cock, none of us talking just seeking our pleasures. He's just as big as Grant, and I love the taste of his dripping cum just as much.

His hips rock as he pumps fast and then slow, holding my head to him. The tug on my hair makes me moan.

Grant picks that moment to spread my virgin hole and tongue fuck me.

"Damn girl, so tight," he mumbles around my pussy lips, making me jerk. My hand shoots to his head and I hold him to me.

"Arg," I cry out, gripping Linc's cock harder in my other hand.

"Ah fuck, man, do whatever you did again, Grant. She likes it," he grunts, and his friend does, making me melt.

I pinch my legs closed around Grant's broad shoulders, "I'm… I'm so close."

Grant lifts his head. "Not yet, baby."

I'm panting and sweating, my heart racing from all the pleasure rolling through me.

Linc pushes up and as if they are in tune with one another, Cain slips his cock from my mouth and turns me to Linc's. I open like the greedy girl I am and suck off the pearls of milky cum leaking from the fat head of his cock before sinking his wide girth into my mouth. He doesn't stop until he hits the back of my throat. I can feel my lips swelling from all the delicious torture they are giving my mouth and I secretly love.

My orgasm rumbles through me, and Linc picks up speed.

"She's a virgin," Grant says, pushing to his knees.

All three kneel over me, and I'm so lost in all the pleasure his words don't hit me at first. "Yes," I confirm, blushing beyond belief.

"Fuck me, our girl waited for us. We have virgin cum on our mouths." Cain wraps his hand around mine and together we start pumping his cock faster.

Grant is back between my legs with Linc on my other side with my other hand.

Together Cain and Linc jerk off over me and they both spill their hot cum on my breasts, their deep, husky shouts sending me over my own edge with the help of Grant's expert tongue.

He flicks over my clit and presses his thumb against my back entrance until I'm blind with the thrill of my release. I rake my nails over his shoulders, my head thrown back with my cry of ecstasy.

It rockets through me forcing me to dig my heels into the mounds of blankets.

And then Grant is over me, cock in hand and I find I can't look away.

His muscled thighs spread my legs wide but for him it's not enough. "Give me room, baby, spread those beautiful fucking legs further. I'm going to come all over that virgin pussy." His command is rough and low, and I can't deny him even if I tried.

I gasp and moan under him as he throws back his head as the first rope of cum lands on my greedy pussy. He rocks his hips as rope after rope spills, and when he's done we both stare at each other. My eyes are wide and his expression is one of complete bliss.

"I wanted that so much," I say before I can stop myself.

They each fall forward, and it's Linc who kisses me first before passing me to Cain. Grant moves in like a bear and claims my lips for himself, making Cain chuckle.

"Look at the animal you've created," he says.

I am and I can't help but wonder at the trouble I've created.

Grant pulls away and holds my eyes with his. The blue is sharp, and he feels delicious with his spent cock pressing against my sticky pussy. "You're beautiful when you come for us. I can't wait to sink my cock into that virgin hole and take you as ours."

"Why wait," I ask as I palm his face gently.

"Because you're not mentally ready to be ours," Cain answers from beside me, and I know he speaks for all of them. They have this very annoying talent of finishing each other's sentences.

"It's bad enough I came all over your bare pussy. I shouldn't have but couldn't hold back."

Linc turns me to look at him. "When we do, it will be just like now, bare, raw and you taking our milk. From ALL three of us."

Oh, God help me, what have I done?

∽

A couple of hours later the men are sprawled out on the sofa and makeshift bed sleeping off the excitement of the early afternoon. The sun has dipped to just past noon, and I'm freshly showered standing in the middle of the messy kitchen.

Once I'd like to enjoy a shower where I'm not so damn mad I almost scrub my skin raw.

I jerk on the water faucet and watch the steamy, hot water pour over the dirty dishes.

Damn men always wanting to be in control. All the talk of home and love. Tears well but I fight them back.

I let the suds build before I set to work cleaning the breakfast dishes. I scrub and then scrub some more and when the plates are washed and dried, I store them in the cabinet the way I want them. Cups over the coffeemaker and plates by the stove. Not how Grant organized them.

I swing open the fridge to put everything back the way I want it, but it seems one of the nosy, know-it-all trio picked up on my system. Dairy top. Meats middle, and all the wine on the bottom.

Tempted to crack open a bottle, I shut the door and pull my hair up in a ponytail instead.

I need a clear mind to handle these three. Plus, I can't drink and drive, and I don't think I plan on sticking around.

I can't. They want what I can't give them. My heart just hurts too much. I'm already a slave to my body when I am around them. I came here to mourn and move on. Not step back into the past and relive old feelings.

I am supposed to be here healing my heart and finding peace, not making out with my crushes from before I understood what wanting three men really meant.

I toss the kitchen towel on the counter and peek in at the men who are all still asleep. I'm by the back door, slipping on a pair of sneakers when big sculpted arms wrap around me, and I'm pulled into a broad chest, all of me melting to all of him.

Lincoln. I know his touch and the light woodsy scent of his by memory. Time could never erase that.

He presses a kiss to the small dip between my shoulder and neck, and my eyes fall closed for a moment, just living in that second.

But it doesn't last and he pulls away, turning me around to look at him.

"Where are you going, sweetheart?" His voice is sleep-heavy.

"I just need some air," I answer.

He pulls me in and presses a light kiss to my still swollen lips, and my hands fall to his bare chest.

"Not now but when you're ready, it's okay to come to us and talk."

I look through the doorway and see Cain and Grant still asleep. "I don't even know where to begin." I shrug.

In the past, Linc always kept to himself, didn't talk much but was always there. He had a troubled childhood and didn't know how to fit in, from what I could understand. We never touched on the topic, but I heard things.

Bringing it up now almost seems cruel, but I have to know how he survived through loss and pain.

I pause.

"Ask me anything you want to know." He rests a hand on my hip, and for a second I wonder how he can read me so easily.

"How did you get past your rough childhood? How did you set aside those demons?"

"You don't know?" He genuinely looks puzzled by my question.

"I had you, your brother, Cain and Grant, and your mom and dad. But most of all, I had you. After a while, I learned how to trust myself to overcome the failings of others all with the help of people who *did* love me. Just like you need to do. You're not alone unless you want to be, sweetheart, and don't think for a second we're going to let you go now that we have you so close. You have us."

I'm stunned into silence. Of all the answers, that is not what I expected.

I slowly nod, not knowing what else to do at not only his admission, but the feelings his words stir inside me.

I turn to the door and slip out of his arms.

"Don't go far."

He reaches for me and caresses a hand across my cheek, and his face softens with the love he keeps speaking about.

I can't quite catch my breath from the intensity.

"I won't," I blurt and then I'm gone.

NINE
CAIN

I nail Linc with a hard look. "You rushed it. We all rushed her. She's not coming back."

I press my back into the hardwood of the kitchen chair and try not to let my emotions cloud my words. But it's not easy. Not with so much at stake.

Grant's sitting across from me, coffee mug in hand. I've never seen him look so worried. Hell, he's gone into gunfights with more hope on his face than he has right now. He rakes his nails across the stubble on his chin. Another sign the man is suffering right along with Linc and me.

He never went a day without shaving, and here he is damn near wearing a full beard.

"Maybe we shouldn't have spanked her. We went too far. She wasn't ready. Shit, then I empty my fucking load on her the way I did." We can all see he's kicking his own ass.

I reach out and clap him on the shoulder, in silent support. I was caught up in the same heat and can understand the torture he's putting himself through.

Lincoln shakes his head. "You guys worry too much. She just needs some air."

I sigh, shoulders slumping. Nah, I don't buy it.

"I thought I was the laid-back one. Since when did you get so damn chill?"

"Since coming here, seeing her. I think half my pent-up need for control was all based on needing her, I swear." He huffs out a big sigh. "Maybe. Hell, I don't know."

"What do you know?" I ask.

"That she won't go far because her hiking shoes are gone by the back door, her laptop is still on the kitchen counter, and she took the southern path that only leads to the secluded wilderness. Plus, she kissed me like a lover does and said she would be back. That's good enough for me."

I snort a short laugh. "You cocky SOB, you could have led with that."

Linc grins. "Seeing you torture yourself was a little bit funny though."

Torture is right. I've agonized over every detail about our shared night seven years ago. I was the one between her legs. The one teasing her into an orgasm and also the one who had to suffer through not tasting those virgin juices back then.

"I can't believe she held out for us."

Linc stretches out looking relaxed, but his words drive a blade in my chest. "It goes deeper than that. She held on because she was afraid of letting someone close. We hurt her, and we need to fix that. If nothing else, we can't let that shit continue. Even if she rejects us."

Grant thumps a fist on the table. "Nah, we can't. But do you think she'll actually turn us away? I thought we weren't letting her leave here until we make sure she knows who she belongs to?" Grant's brows are pinched, and I can tell he's about to raise some hell. He hasn't exactly been the quiet type when it comes to Mercy. The big boy has his heart set on keeping our girl for ourselves.

The room goes silent.

"Me too." I finally answer. "But if she wants to walk, I'm not going to lock her away. I could never do that to her. I know you couldn't either. Neither of you."

"Yeah." Grant rubs a hand around his neck. "So let's give her no other choice but to stay."

I'm quiet a second before I say, "I saw a look of uncertainty in her eyes when you told her how things would go down between all of us."

"Shit," Grant grumbles. He holds up both hands like he thinks there is no other choice to make. "She needed to know."

Up until then, Linc has been quiet. "She's still holding back from us. We have to dig deeper to help her see what we want isn't some backwoods fuck fest where no one can see us and then it's all over once we are back in the real world."

Grant finishes off his coffee and walks it to the sink and rinses. "We should go after her. What if she gets lost or comes across a cougar or something? Plus, it will be dark soon."

Linc jerks a thumb toward our buddy. "I think Grant is right." Changing his laid-back routine all of a sudden.

I shake my head. "Listen, you two, I don't think she particularly likes the caveman routine you pulled on her today, and she grew up in these woods." I can't believe what I am saying when five minutes ago I would have been on Grant's side and all three of us would be charging out of here like possessed demons on the hunt. "She's not going to get lost. Like you said, she knows these woods. And," I crack a grin, "throwing her over your shoulder might have worked once but do it again, and I'm not going to stand in the way when she wants to knee you in the nuts."

"So now we get a plan worked up." Grant is leaning against the counter, arms crossed like a roughed-up bear.

I nod. "Now we're on the same page."

Linc moves to the coffeepot and puts on a fresh brew, bypassing the whiskey we all would prefer.

Linc cranks an eyebrow at me in question.

"That's for after we get the girl. I have a few ideas that will get Mercy's attention once and for all. This afternoon we showed her the tip of what it will be like having three men devoted to her. Now we need to prove she's more than a backwoods fling for us. That she's our forever. Period."

Grant and Linc have only one answer. "I'm in."

TEN
MERCY

Y*ou have us.*

"What did he mean by that? Today was supposed to be about sex. Get it out of my system and move on. But now? Now everything is complicated and matted together."

I'm so angry they forced a confession of my feelings, but at the same time, I feel a peace I haven't felt in years. They are only trying to help, but on the flip side, I wasn't ready.

Why? "Isn't that what you are here for?" I demand of myself.

Tingles are still shooting through me, and it's been hours since they've touched me.

And Lincoln's last words were so heartfelt. He still carried pain. I saw it, didn't I? But he smiles and laughs like someone who has found peace. I want that.

So then why am I fighting it?

TEN

I find a large boulder by the lake's edge and spread out on the big expanse, soaking up the late afternoon rays. Because I'm scared.

I don't know where the words come from but they are whispered across my mind as if I spoke them verbally.

I ball my fists, rear my head back and let out a belly full of angst with a roar. Birds scatter, and a few ducks along the water's edge fly away, leaving me in silence.

A light wind comes up off the lake to flutter through the trees. And with it, I notice two things. The world still rotates, and I suddenly feel better.

Life moves on. Out here so close to the places my brother loved, I can feel him, and a serene peace comes over me. Just like I need to. Just like Lincoln said.

I laugh softly. The answer was always there right in front of my eyes, only I was too blind to see it.

Maybe healing isn't about sweating it out and forcing the pain to move on or else. Like I have some kind of control. Maybe I need to learn how to live with it, embrace it and learn to live and love?

I sit up and wrap my arms around my knees. Grant, Cain and Lincoln are not the problems. I'm my own problem, and all of a sudden, I feel like kicking my own ass. The guys were right. They didn't say it in so many words, but I know what they meant. I've been selfish to think I'm the only one in pain.

I take out my phone and snap a few pictures of the calm waters and then a selfie just as the sun meets the horizon and shoot them off with a quick text to my mom and dad.

. . .

"*Love you guys bunches, all is good and no crazy man living in the cabin eating roadkill*"

Just three crazy, insanely hot men I'm silly stupid crazy about. But it's probably better I break that particular news in person.

A ding comes back.

"*Send our love to the boys*"

I smile as I read my mom's text. She knew all along. I've been not only blind but stupid too. I hope they haven't left. Suddenly, my heart squeezes until I can't breathe.

I've been sitting here lost in thought longer than expected. Fireflies begin to dance along the tree line and over the yard as I step off the hiking path that comes out opposite the cabin. They look like fallen stars blinking over the water making it look like this tiny slice of heaven is a hidden portal to the whole universe laid out before me.

Amazing what a few orgasms, kind words and love can do for a girl. My perspective has had a rude awakening.

Crossing the yard with my head down, lost in thought, at first I don't see the lights. A warm glow brings my attention, and I blink several times in awe.

TEN

A huge blanket is spread out over the grass with a wide view of the lake before us and the stars above. Hanging overhead are string lights they must have dug out of the hall storage. Their soft glow a warm highlight over what looks like a beautiful spread they prepared.

Cain appears to my right, taking my hand in his larger one. "I hope you still like your dessert before dinner, Mercy baby."

And for a second I think he's talking about another soul-shattering orgasm, and I blush. He leans forward. "That's coming too, baby. Just wait."

"Where is everyone?" I look around for Linc and Grant, but I don't see anyone.

"Do you remember when we asked you to be patient that night you asked us to take your virginity?"

It takes me a minute before I nod. "I do. You all told me no one would understand and that I would be shunned for my desires, and you didn't want that for me. You didn't want me growing up too fast when all I wanted was the three of you."

Cain's eyes light up with a hunger I've only dreamed about seeing in his eyes. "Such a brave girl."

I tighten my fingers around his. "I was never afraid. I knew what I wanted."

"And now?"

Cain looks down at me, waiting patiently for my answer.

"I think I have an answer for that now."

He leads me over to the blankets and draws me over his lap. He's freshly showered with loose shorts and a T-shirt stretched over broad shoulders, his feet bare. Like he's home. And that thought has my heart swelling.

I wrap my arms around his neck and press close enough to where my nipples are rubbing against his chest through the soft material of my tank top. Thankfully I packed several of them. Those and panties, because between these three I never have a dry pair. A stiff wind and my skirt would reveal that truth pretty quickly.

"What is all this about?" I ask, nodding to the variety of delicious smelling fresh fruit, a bowl of whipped cream, chilled wine I notice and, is that a bottle of lube? I stiffen a little at that.

He moves my hair over my shoulder and he takes a moment to gather his thoughts.

"You know the three of us wanted nothing more than to take you right in the middle of your kitchen that night. We couldn't do that to you. Not Grant, Linc or me. Please understand that."

"I do," I say. "I was being selfish and blind, but I see it now and I'm not mad. I didn't want to see that you did it because you cherished me enough to let me grow up a little before I did something I might regret. I understand why you waited."

"And do you regret it?" he asks somberly, and I know my next words have to be measured because Cain might be a Marine and a man accustomed to fighting his way through conflict, but he's also the softest of the three men when it comes to me. It's written all over his face.

"No," I say. "I only regret it took me so long to see how much you three love me. But I regret more not telling you all first."

TEN

His hands go to the back of my head and his lips are on mine in a fiery kiss that turns slow and possessive.

I pull away. "And I know why you guys waited so long for me. I wasn't ready. Grant was right."

"Hmm-hmm. You needed space to figure out your own life before we complicated it with the three of us. Hell, so did we. We've always known we would share the one woman who we eventually ended up with, but that's still not something that is easy to wrap around the brain. Linc was pretty messed up about it and his family didn't help. Told him he was fucked up in the head and a perverted son of a bitch, and it only gets worse but you get the idea. He had a lot of shit to work out. Then add on top of that shit pile the very real possibility one of us could get killed. We didn't want to burden you with that."

"And now? What's changed?"

"We don't give a damn anymore. Selfish as that is. Either the other people in our lives will learn to live with our life choices or they won't," Cain adds almost as an afterthought. "Either way we can live with as long as you are in our lives."

I stay silent for a moment.

"Talk to me, baby. What's going on in that mind of yours. Please don't hold back anymore."

"I've held onto so much pain in my heart that I'm finding it hard to do what I always dreamed about. Before Jake died, I thought I could find someone to be happy with. Thought you guys didn't want me. But it never happened. I tried, but when they saw I couldn't love them back, they rejected me like trash. I can't blame them really. But after Jake… it felt like my world stopped rotating. I didn't have him and I didn't have the three of you. I thought traveling, getting out there and seeing other people being happy, I could find mine. Stupid, I know, but I didn't know what else to do."

"You needed to come home to us. You had us. You always will have us. You didn't want to see that for some reason, but I hope you do now."

"I do." I pause a moment to gather my thoughts and soak in the way he's caressing my face. I close my eyes. "It's why I came here. I thought I could sweat out the pain, you know? I can't live the life I want. I can't tell the beautiful stories of love and hope and joy to children through my stories until I find a way past all this. Maybe I'm not destined to be an author. Maybe I'm meant to be an illustrator for others who can share all those things with others through their words."

He runs a hand over my hair and scoots me closer until I wrap my legs around him.

His cock is hard and pressing into the soft fabric of my panties, the skirt I shimmied into earlier after our afternoon fun riding high.

I gasp. "Cain!"

"Tell me, is writing and painting all you want out of life? Or do you want something more?"

"More. I want something more. I want the people I love by my side to share it with," I say breathlessly.

"Good girl." He rubs the tips of our noses together.

"I knew from the first time I saw you, Linc and Cain there was something special between us."

"We knew it, too, sweetheart," Grant walks over and sits beside me. "We knew it, but you were too young, too innocent for the three of us."

Linc joins us a second later and kneels behind me. "We couldn't taint you with our perverted ways."

"And now?" I say in a teasing voice.

"Oh baby, you're in trouble now. You're all ours and there's no saving you from all the filthy things we're going to do to you."

ELEVEN
MERCY

Cain strips off his shirt, and Linc and Grant follow. I look around but see no one and remember there's not another soul for miles.

"What are you doing?"

My heart starts to race. I know what is coming, hope Grant keeps his word.

"We're going to show you the world, baby." Linc hauls me up and off Cain's lap, and I turn to see him stripping his clothes off until he's bare, hard cock in hand.

Grant is next. He's pulling off his shorts and tossing them to the side.

That leaves Lincoln.

I walk up to him and take the hem of his shorts in hand. "Allow me," and I'm on my knees taking his shorts with me. His thick cock bounces in front of me as I pull it free and I wrap my fingers around his massive thickness. Looking up, I sink my mouth over the fat head, working my tongue in a little swallowing effect as I deep throat him.

From behind me Cain is pulling my tank over my head, and I slip Linc from my mouth only long enough for Cain to toss the blouse to the side. I palm my tits and groan around his throbbing, veined cock as I squeeze my candy-hard nipples.

I press my hands to his abs, his rippling muscle strained. He groans and rocks his hips a little faster. "Fuck, your mouth is so fucking perfect," he husks.

"Mercy baby, squeeze those hard tips again, for him." Grant is on his knees beside me, unhooking the buttons and zipper holding my skirt in place. It slips to the floor to stop at my knees along with the thong tucked between my ass cheeks.

I gasp, and Linc drives his cock deeper.

"Naughty, dirty little girl. Next time, when we have more time to play I'm going to pull these off with my teeth inch by inch."

I shiver from the whispered promise. "Yes, please," I say and hold his gaze for a heated moment. His blue eyes flame with the same fire I feel in me. The longer he looks at me the hotter it becomes.

I can feel Grant's cock throbbing against my thigh. He cups my breast and pinches and tugs at one nipple. Cain is on the other side doing the same.

"Moan for me, baby," he purrs close to my ear and I do. I can't help it or the flush that blooms across my cheeks.

"I want you on your knees now, baby," Grant growls, and Linc pulls his dick from between my lips with a sloppy pop.

I nod slowly. My nipples harden even more at his command, and I fall to my hands and knees, pressing my ass in the air.

Blood rushes through my veins so fast I can hear the thunder in my ears.

Grant flips me over on my back and spreads my legs with his hard, chiseled thighs. I'm spread so wide all of me can be seen by the three of them. "Grant is going to take that pretty pussy first, and then I'll be taking that virgin ass."

Cain taking my ass makes me clench. Would he fit? The burn of having two take me sends a thrill shooting from head to toe.

I never thought about who would be taking me first, but it makes sense that Grant would be the one. I fell in love with him first, and then on the heels of that truth came my affection and love for Cain and Linc. All inside a week, but still Grant was first.

Grant slides a finger through my juices and then eases a finger into my tight hole.

I start to breathe hard, and Linc leans over, devouring one nipple with his hot mouth, and Cain takes the other. I bury my hands in their hair and lock eyes with Grant as he inserts another finger, stretching me for his thick cock.

I cry out, "I need you. Now, Grant, I need you."

Knowing Cain and Linc hear me beg makes the fire in me burn hotter. They release my nipples and lean back on their heels, watching Grant guide his cock to my entrance. I reach for them, and they take my hands.

"Watch him take you, baby," Linc gruffs in a deep voice.

Grant takes his cock in hand and guides it to my impossibly tight hole.

"This will hurt but only a little, and then we'll take the pain away."

"I trust you."

Oh God, this is all about to happen. Everything I've ever wanted is coming true.

My arms ache to hold him. To feel his weight on me, holding me down.

As if reading my mind, he falls forward on his elbows and takes my mouth with his as he claims my body. I wrap my legs around him and press my heels into the flesh of his ass, not wanting him to wait. I want to feel every last burn and thrust of him. To feel is to be alive, and that's how they make me feel.

"Do it," I demand.

He hesitates slightly before breaking through my innocence with one powerful thrust and making me his.

I cry out, "Yes!" My head thrashes, and a part of me heals in that instant.

He stills, breathing heavily over me, his forehead pressed against mine. "I'm so *so* sorry, baby. Forgive me for hurting you like that."

I take his face between my hands. "It doesn't hurt, not anymore," I say, and he looks into my eyes as if searching for the truth.

Satisfied, he rocks his hips gently at first and then he picks up speed, spreading my tight walls to better fit his big size. He's pounding my pussy, fucking me hard, when Linc kneels by my mouth and slips his cum-soaked cock head over my pouty lips. I open for him, he sinks in, and I take him as deep as I can.

It's not enough. I whimper, needing even more. Not quite feeling whole yet.

I reach for Cain, and he takes my hand guiding me to his shaft. I stroke tip to base, running my thumb over the sticky, wet head.

Grant rises to his knees, gripping my hips with his powerful hands, pumping hard and fast.

I release Linc just as my vision blurs and my orgasm splinters through me hotter than lightning.

Grant pulls his spent cock from me, my silky soft walls still pulsating from my orgasm, when Cain is between my legs and flipping me over.

Cain runs his hands over my bare ass, and I know he's watching his friend's cum drip from my newly fucked hole.

He slips his fingers through my slit to find my clit and circles it once. Twice. I peer over my shoulder on the third time, pressing back, eager for the dark promises in Cain's eyes.

Linc pulls me back and slides his dick back into my mouth. "Take me now, baby."

He pumps, holding my head steady with a hand buried in my hair. Arms shaking, I hollow my lips but I'm not ready for the heady, earthy taste of his cum on my tongue. He fists his balls and empties his load, and I can't swallow fast enough. Milky cum slips from my lips, and he catches the rivulets, bringing them back to my lips for me to lick off his cock head.

"Mmm," I moan, craving more.

"That's it, baby, take all of me. Don't waste a drop."

I knew it was coming, knew what was about to happen, but I'm still shocked when Cain trails his fingers through mine and Grant's cum to rub it over my ass. He flexes his fingers in the flesh of my ass and parts me farther.

Cain nudges my cunt and then sinks in, my primed pussy ready. I clench around the intrusion, welcoming the sudden fullness. He wraps a strong arm around my waist and drives in so hard I nearly lose my mind.

He does it again, and on the third time he pulls out, pressing the tip of his cock to my back entrance.

"Ready for me to pop the cherry ass, baby?" The tone of his voice says he's ready, but my body starts to tremble.

"We've got you, baby. We'd never do anything you don't want." Grant is by my side whispering in my ear. Only the crickets and the soft sound of water on the shore can be heard as they wait for my answer.

On my elbows, I turn to hold his gaze and smile. "I never want to hold back with any of you."

That's all he needed. My dominant Marine breaks through the last of my barriers.

Linc trails kisses over my shoulder, and Grant reaches between my legs, working my clit with the pad of his finger. Years of rough work have toughened his fingers, and the second he touches me, I'm damn near seeing fireworks. I clench my eyes closed, panting hard.

Inch by slow inch, Cain sinks his shaft into my ass. I scream from all the sensations bombarding me at once. I can't focus on any of them. They are that strong and overwhelming.

I'm panting and barely holding on when Cain pulls out only to glide back in and starts fucking my ass.

"Making you ours has been our goal for years, baby girl. Now you'll never know the touch of another man."

"I only want the three of you. No one else."

He pulls out, Grant right there stroking my clit. My head is spinning, and my whole world is about to cave in. Cain picks up speed, flexing and massaging my ass as he takes me slow one second fast and hard the next.

I gasp when his cock swells and he clamps a strong arm around my waist again.

Fire is burning every nerve ending, and I'm so close I don't know if I can hold on. My walls clench and my ass tightens.

"Fuck," Cain growls. "You're getting me. That's it, milk my cock. Take me, baby, take all of me."

Linc's lips crash into mine, and he swallows my screams as my own release slams into me hard. Hot seed spills into my ass, Cain's cock jerking again and again.

Harsh breaths rip from my lips as Lincoln releases my mouth. "You are beautiful, baby," he whispers for only me and I smile resting my head on his forearm.

"Now I feel whole," I say just loud enough for all three to hear me.

Cain slips from me, taking his shirt to wipe me clean.

But I don't get much of a rest.

Grant picks me up, and I have my legs wrapped around his hips. His cock slips between my flushed and pleasured folds, and I groan when his cock nudges my swollen clit.

"What's wrong, baby? You still need more?"

I nod. All of a sudden feeling ravenous.

He wraps a massive arm around my waist, lifts and I sink down on his hard cock, taking every single inch until he's fully seated inside me.

"God, baby, any less of a man would cum the second those lips sucked their cock in like that."

"But I have you," I say, "and Linc and Cain."

"Yes, you do."

Each of them kisses me before Grant stands, taking me with him.

He smirks, that delicious mouth of his tempting me closer again. I love the feel of his beard against my skin and wonder if I'll ever have enough of these three in this lifetime. "You don't think the night is over, do you? We have something else in store for you."

We storm through the house, Grant's cock still buried deep in my pussy. I clench and shimmy my hips as he carries me through the house. Fucking him as he walks turns out to be harder than I thought, but we manage. Barely.

My candles are lit and scattered here and there, but the important ones are all lined up the edges of the stairs and down the hall, leading the way to the master suite.

For a second, I don't know what to say. They put a lot of thought into tonight and all for me.

I bury my hands in Grant's hair and devour his mouth. He parts for me, and I dive in, craving the taste of him.

Linc flings the door open and Grant tosses me on the bed. Standing in front of me are my three men lined up like wolves ready to eat their Red Riding Hood.

"Well, come on, boys." I smile, spreading my thighs. A hint of my virgin blood marks my thighs but that only turns them on more. All three have cocks in hand, the heavy weight ready.

"Looks like I'm not the only one ready for round two." I pull on a sassy grin, "Only I'm on top this time."

Linc's brows raise, and Grant and Cain chuckle.

"We'll see about that, Mercy baby. We'll see about that."

As all three descend on me, ravishing me in their own special way, I've never felt more at home. In their arms, in their hearts, I know this is where I am meant to be.

"I love you," I whisper. I know the first time I say it I have to tell them together, and just as I thought, all three pause and hold my gaze one at a time.

"And we adore you, baby," Linc says.

Grant clears his throat. "There was a time I thought none of us would hear those words from you." He smiles the kind of smile that reaches into those crystal blue eyes. "I love you more than life."

"You *are* our lives, Mercy baby." Cain turns those green eyes on me, and I cradle his face close to mine, feeling completely whole.

"I believe you. I had no idea how long I was holding my breath until I saw you all standing in my doorway again. I'd grown so used to the pain I just thought it was how life was supposed to feel."

"Mercy baby, seven years is a long time to hold your breath. And it might not seem like it, but we feel the same. We forgot how to live until you came back into our lives."

"You'll never have to go without us again."

"That's a promise."

And then they seal it with a soul-searing kiss I'll never forget.

They move together like a machine. One taking over where the other leaves off, loving every inch of my body. Knowing what the other wants and thinks. Having all that attention aimed at me leaves me more than just a little breathless. I'm lost in it and I don't think I ever want to be found if this is what being loved by three alpha men is like.

EPILOGUE
MERCY

My heart squeezes when I hear a small cough from the door at my back. It's been three years and I still get goosebumps when one of my husbands catches me going down on one of the others.

What can I say? I like the thrill *and* the teasing them tends to make the sex all the hotter.

I swivel my head just enough to where Grant's cock doesn't slip free of my mouth, and I freeze as a set of sea-green eyes locks on mine.

This is the last weekend we'll have of just the four of us at the cabin and our surrounding fifty acres. It's taken almost the full three years to put it all into action, but my three men have all retired from the military and have set up their own lakeside boating business and cabin rental. Come Monday, Lucky Three Lakeside Retreat is officially open for business and the bookings are already filled to the max. My parents were more than happy to sell us the cabin and see us all start to build our new lives together.

"Tell me something, Mercy baby, did you really think you could kiss me hello in the kitchen and then five minutes later slide that delicious mouth over my friend's cock and me not know about it?"

I smile around Grant's cock. Busted. I don't entirely have an answer that won't end up with me having red ass cheeks, so I continue enjoying my feast. I tighten my fingers around Grant's muscled thighs and noisily suck. From the corner of my eye, I see what it's doing to Cain, and I have a hard time not smiling.

From my position on my knees, I raise my gaze up to see Grant's amazingly blue eyes and for a second, I'm taken back to the night he claimed my virginity. He had the same possessive look of love then as he does now as he stares down at me.

Grant chuckles deeply, and I love the roughness of it. Always have.

"Answer him, sweetheart," he urges quietly, "I have to say, I'm curious too."

I reluctantly pull back, causing the heavy weight of Grant's cock to slip from my mouth with a juicy, wet pop. "I was hungry and feeling all alone up here in the house while you three worked." Which is a lie. I was with them all day helping out when I could, and I haven't been up here fifteen minutes, but I'm horny and want my husbands' attention all to myself.

"Grant was already naked from his shower and I swear I saw cum on his dick that needed cleaning." I lean in and suck him clean of the cum dripping from his cock head. "See? Besides, I didn't tell him to walk through the house butt ass naked like a walking fantasy." I give a shrug and turn a little to see Cain leaning against the doorframe, arms crossed and a cocky grin on his lips. In one hand he has a jar of my mom's homemade peach jam and the wicked glint in his eyes has my whole body going on full alert.

"Before your mom left with the kids, she gave us a little present." He wiggles the jar in the air. "There's a whole case of this out on the porch. "The boys and I've already had a little, but there's a special little something we want to go with our next helping."

Me. I'm that special something. My chest tightens as a wave of goosebumps spreads all over me.

Some things were just meant to be, and this life taught me that lesson in spades. Like I was meant to be shared between three men. In specific *my* three men and I'm right where I should be.

"I'm hungry too," I say shakily.

Grant takes my chin in his hand, and I see the same burning lust for me as I have for them. "Exactly how hungry are you?" he whispers, guiding the tip of his cum-covered dick over my lips and spreading his hot seed with each pass.

I hear more than see when Linc walks into the house. Licking my lips, I turn to find droplets of water glittering in his dark hair fall to his shoulders and glide over hard muscles. Obviously, he hosed off outside before coming in and conveniently left off the clothes, I notice. Someone has big ears, I quietly muse to myself. Because his beautiful, perfectly veined shaft is hard and ready for me.

Sweet heaven.

I'd teased the hell out of them all day in my skimpy two-piece thong bikini. A black and pink number that had their jeans bulging all day. It seems I might be about to pay for my sins and they've kept a tally of my transgressions.

EPILOGUE

The walls of my pussy clench, forcing the hot liquid to spill over and wet my thighs.

Linc growls deep in his throat, and I know the look in each of their eyes. It means I'm in big trouble. The delicious, sinful kind that will make a priest blush hotter than I am right now.

Cain pushes his large body from the kitchen doorframe and pulls his T-shirt off to reveal exquisitely tanned skin. He's been outside all day with Grant and Linc reinforcing the new boat dock after heavy rains and the results have me licking my lips and smiling in appreciation.

Holy cow the tingles and anticipation of feeling all that against all of me haven't faded and I know it never will.

"I'll never get tired of seeing you want me so much." I can't help but say what I'm feeling for them. Letting them into my heart and sharing my true feelings didn't come easy, but I've grown under their love and care. And they've done the same.

Linc and Cain stroll across the living room, with Cain tossing his shirt aside and kicking off his boots.

His jeans come off and join the pile of clothing.

In seconds all three are standing over me—dominant, alpha as fuck and horny, their dicks solid as steel.

I should have run off. Played a little harder to get and let them catch me. Maybe I should have at least tried to explain how I ended up on my knees three seconds after kissing Cain in the kitchen, but I can't help but feel turned on knowing Cain and Linc witnessed me pleasuring their best friend. Frankly, still doing, since my lips are back on Grant's cock kissing and teasing. I wrap my hands around the thick, heavy weight. Truth is, I planned this whole weekend while my parents visit their one-year-old grandbabies. The twins have been a handful, and I'm grateful for the family support. We don't get a lot of time together, so I'm going to make sure we all enjoy every second we have. Not only this weekend but forever.

Back-to-back deadlines with my publisher have kept me busy too, and it's time we all stepped back and appreciated life.

Holding Cain's gaze, I reach up and wrap my fingers around Grant's dick with one hand and cup his balls in the other, rolling them as I sink my mouth around his thick girth.

"Fuck me, that's gorgeous. Are you looking for another spanking?" Linc sinks his naked body onto the sofa and drags me from Grant, spreading me out over his lap ass up.

Cain moves in behind me, sliding his hands over my silky skin, touching me everywhere like he's worshipping me. Grant's teeth are at the strings of my bikini top and when he pulls, my nipples slip free, candy hard and needy. He bends and suckles a hard tip between his lips, and I gasp, arching, giving Linc access to pinch the other just right to make the tingling in my core burn hotter.

I reach out and run the tips of my fingers over Grant's gorgeous muscle, and he groans for me just the way I like to hear. He glides his hands down my back, nibbling over my bare shoulder, and Cain lifts the taut strings of my thong around my hips for Grant to untie.

One tug and Cain slowly peels the strip from between my cheeks. "Ahh," I arch and press back into Cain.

I gasp when something moist and sticky is spread over my ass and... "Oh my God, what are you doing?" I turn to see a sly smile lift Cain's lips a moment before he licks them with a smack.

"Making our peach of a pussy all the sweeter."

Grant's large fingers spread me wide, and Cain smears another healthy dose of jam over my folds.

I can't help the moan that slips out, and I try to wiggle a little, but Linc clamps a strong arm around my middle. "Shh, baby, you're not the only one hungry. Let your men eat." He feels sun-warmed against me and the jerk of his cock nudging my tummy makes me want a taste of my own.

From beside me, Grant flexes his fingers into the flesh of my ass and holds me wide for his hungry friend. Cain's tongue swirls over my tight little asshole, and then he dips lower, sucking and licking until I feel like I'm going to come just by him eating me out.

"That's it, baby, let them love you," Linc purrs.

I often wondered if I'd ever find happiness and I think that's been answered threefold. I feel so loved, lusted over and naughty all at once. Like I'm their dirty angel.

Cain slips a finger in and then two stroking my walls, curling against my G-spot. In front of me, Grant strokes his beautiful, throbbing cock and glides the fat tip to my lips. I open wide for him. He sinks in, and I feel how badly he needs to come. His balls are heavy with his release and I can't wait until he gives it all to me.

I hollow my cheeks around his shaft as he sinks deeper, filling my mouth.

Linc caresses a hand over my back, tracing the delicate outline of my spine just before slipping between my ass cheeks as Cain replaces his fingers with his shaft. He presses against me, easing just the head in. I can feel him pulsating and I push back.

He playfully slaps my ass. "Greedy as always."

My velvety walls stretch to accommodate his thickness, and my juices wet us both, allowing him to sink in until his balls bounce lightly against my clit.

Linc's naughty fingers circle around my tight back entrance, and he barely breaches me when Cain grips my hips and starts to fuck me harder.

Pleasure builds and it's about to overflow into a sizzling orgasm. I clench my walls and my mouth, wanting my men's milk as it hits. I gasp around Grant's shaft right before he pulls out, his cock still angry and hard. My body tenses and I reach for my nipples as Linc pushes his finger deeper into my ass, spreading me. Suddenly the sizzles turn into a raging fire. My orgasm must have sent Cain over the edge too. I can feel him jerk inside me and his hot spurts of cum spill into me. But before I can float down, Grant hauls me up from Linc's lap, and I'm turned around with my back to Linc and my legs pinned open.

He eases my freshly fucked slit over his hard cock and thrusts into me once, twice. "Lincoln," I cry out, wanting him to go faster. I'm burning up and I can already feel another release building. Grant is in front of me holding me to his chest as his friend pulls out, leaving only the crown of his cock to tease my entrance before he drives back into me. Then Linc pulls his soaked shaft out, and he presses the head to my back entrance.

My heart is pounding, and I'm breathing heavily. Grant's strong hands are on my hips as he guides me to sink my ass over my husband's shaft. I moan so loud I think our neighbors ten miles down the road can hear the amount of pleasure pumping through me.

Linc moves to the edge of the cushion, and Grant pushes between my legs and fills me up. Both take me as Cain watches, stroking his cock, which is already getting hard for me.

Pinned between Linc and Grant, they work together, pushing me higher and higher until I can't take it anymore. My body shakes and quivers, and I'm so close. Both men hold me tight and our bodies mold like we're meant to fit together.

"So fucking tight and hungry for our cocks," Grant growls, claiming my lips in a hard kiss. His tongue pushes in as he works my pussy, our hearts hammering in rhythm.

He pulls back. "Come for us, baby, milk our cocks so we can do it all over again."

"And again." Linc clamps his hands around my hips and drives in deeper, pleasuring me with just the right amount of force to have me bucking in their arms. My dripping pussy wets all of us and the delicious juicy sounds of my men enjoying me fill my heart until I'm overflowing with love.

"We plan on having our girl all night," Cain adds.

I bury my hands in Grant's hair and pull him closer as I fall back into Linc's arms, who wraps us together in his arms.

A few more strokes of them buried deep in me and my ass clamps down on Linc's cock, and Grant grunts when the walls of my pussy do the same.

"Spread those legs, baby. Let Grant see you come for us." Linc groans gruffly in my ear.

I cry out with pleasure and whimper when they pick up speed. Cain reaches between us and the second his finger finds my swollen pleasure nub, I tumble into my second orgasm, knowing it won't be my last. My whole body shakes and trembles with the power of my release, and my men are there to hold me and keep me safe in their powerful arms.

Linc's throbbing cock is the first to shoot off, and I clamp around him, rocking my hips, taking all of him for myself. He's right. They all are. I'm greedy with what is mine.

Grant throws his head back, shouting his own release, slowly coming to a stop.

God, I love it when they take me like they're starving men. I relax into Linc's arms and just lie there for a second trying to figure out what planet I'm on when the front door crashes in and a loud rumbling roar rocks the inside of the cabin. At first, all I can do is gasp at the sight of a huge brown bear lumbering through the door.

"Oh shit!" Linc has me off his lap and the three of them form a wall of protective muscle in front of me in less than three seconds. I swear once a Marine, right?

Well, I wish I could say I know what happens next but the truth of the matter is it all happens so fast.

Linc dives for an oar hanging on the wall over the couch. Grant growls and waves his hands around like some lunatic while Cain shuffles a chair toward the massive animal.

He rears up on his hind legs and that's when I see it. Jam. It's all over the porch and sticking to paws big enough to give anyone a permanent facial.

Holy shit.

The men start to push the animal out the door but the bear isn't having it. Not when he smells fresh jam. On me.

Oh shit times two.

EPILOGUE

The nine-hundred-pound animal smashes into the kitchen table and it's only a matter of time before he reaches me.

I go to launch myself over the couch, but a pair of arms stop me cold. "Woman, what have we talked about? We protect you. Now stay behind us and no arguing."

"I know but it's not my fault you took out the jam and used me like a piece of bread for dessert between the three of you."

They don't hear me because all three are working as a team to corral the animal back out the door. Cain catches the bear's attention by throwing the open jar outside while Linc shuffles me to the back of the living room and away from danger.

"Thank fuck," Cain gruffs out, looking a little white in the face. "Who left the door open anyway?"

Grant levels his gaze on Linc. "The same dumbass who left jars of jelly on the front porch. Open, might I add."

Linc scrapes a hand over his face. "Shit, I got distracted. And I was just being prepared." He holds me against his body and presses a kiss to the top of my head.

He sits and my heart is still racing as he pulls me onto his lap. His hold is just a little too tight, but I don't say anything, loving how protective my alpha man is over me. "I almost died seeing you in danger."

"Fuck, we all did. My heart nearly gave out." Grant's expression is pinched with worry.

"If we lost you it would be the end of us." Linc presses his forehead against mine and strokes my hair gently.

Grant and Cain join us after securing the door and the secondary door they installed to prevent just that from happening.

"Lost me? It's going to take more than a little ol' bear for that," I tease, pulling back, lightening the mood. The look of horror on Linc's face has my head falling back and me howling with laughter.

All three men's brows are pinched tight. "What's so funny?" Cain asks.

"You three. Okay, so a bear *is* a big deal, but seeing you three turn into Rambo *while* naked…" I cock a half grin and *tsk*. "Let's just say the sight was something to behold."

All three men stand and pass me around, kissing me senseless until I end up in Grant's strong arms.

He taps the end of my nose with his finger. "I swear tomorrow morning I'm installing ten-foot fences around the yard to protect the babies and you."

I can already see Grant's mind at work with the mental blueprint. I take his face between my palms. "Not tonight, nor tomorrow. You can go Robo-Daddy after Sunday. I want all your focus on finding a creative way of using the last jar of jam on me." I point at one out on the porch that miraculously survived tonight's funfest.

"Yes, ma'am," he groans against my lips.

Grant pins me against his chest. "I think we need to go see about making baby number three. Maybe this time it will be a girl."

Linc is already at the foot of the stairs. "Lord help us all if she's anything like her mother."

I laugh. "She'll be blessed and cursed. Two older brothers and three protective daddies. Hmm, I almost feel sorry for the five of you, come to think about it."

A little princess of the house would be a perfect addition to the family, and we all have more than enough love to spread around if we're so blessed.

I turn in Grant's arms and hold my arms open for Cain and Lincoln to press into my sides. Grant holds me tight as all three of my men wrap me in their arms.

"I love you. All of you," and I stop there, feeling my emotions welling up. I don't want to cry and ruin the moment.

"You're our home, Mercy baby."

"Our forever," Linc murmurs against my lips before kissing me sweetly.

"As long as you'll have us, sweetheart."

My heart squeezes. Oh, I'm going to spend the rest of my life and theirs, showing them just how perfect we are together and how much family and love mean. They once thought they were freaks and perverts but they just needed the right woman to unite them, and I'm blessed to be the one.

∽

Thank you for reading, Mercy for Three! Read on for the first chapter of the next book in the series, Honor for Three.

Available on Amazon, Kindle Unlimited & print.

Temptation comes in threes. Three bodyguards that is. First time failed, but they're back to take what they want. Me.

Chapter One
Honor

Not one. Not two, but three gorgeous men wait for me downstairs.

Army Rangers to the core, which means rule-followers through and through when all I want to do is break every last one that keeps them from claiming me in ways I've only fantasized about.

Standing in the middle of my bedroom I mentally run through my game plan one more time.

Limo arrives, share a little birthday champagne, slip my dress off and let my dream fantasy—aka my three über-hot, much older bodyguards—ravish my starved, virgin body.

And then it's happy birthday to me!

EPILOGUE

A shiver works its way through my core and teases my senses until my nipples tighten into hard peaks and I clench my thighs. Suffice to say, getting my cherry popped by three former Rangers is my fantasy come true. I'm equal parts nervous and excited.

Maybe it's not the most detailed of tactics or the most sophisticated, but I know what I want and I'm rolling with it for the first time in my life. Up until this second, it's all been about keeping the family's name pristine and exemplary.

But what happens tonight behind closed doors will stay that way.

My heart races, and I push down the heat coloring my revealing Irish skin. I swear I can't have a single thought without it giving my emotional state away like a flashing billboard.

"I got this. I *can* do this," I pump myself up.

I *have* to do this. How many times have I chickened out before? Too many is how many.

So, no more running scared. Besides, a girl only turns twenty-one once, and I've wanted them for so long I think I've been in a perpetual state of arousal since my father hired them on my eighteenth birthday after a threat on my life nearly took me from him.

The man meant well, but he also crafted a life of torture for his only daughter.

If I don't get their hands on me and soon, I'm afraid I'll either pass out or snap, rip off my clothes and jump them in the middle of some event like a horny, rabid woman.

Surprise! Wouldn't social media love that?

But where would that leave me? Locked up for indecent exposure at the very least, for one. My father's face would be splashed all over the tabloids as a runner-up to my arrest, and wouldn't all of his political rivals love that circus show.

I shudder at the possible headlines. I can't do that to the man who supported me through pimples, my punk rocker phase complete with purple hair and college.

But I also can't ignore how I feel, either.

There's no real fair ground here. Honestly, I don't know what the heck the man was thinking when he walked my new protection detail into his office and introduced me to three of the most gorgeous men I've ever seen. I've never lusted over a single guy before let alone three, but here I am, wet and ready for anything they want from me.

Smooth silk glides over my curves as I shimmy into a dress that practically doubles as a shirt made from what feels like weightless clouds, I swear. It certainly is the shade of the sky after a summer rain and the storm has cleared. The color plays well with my citrine eyes and makes my creamy skin stand out.

I waffled between this one and a floor-length black number featuring a scandalous double thigh-high slit that reveals more skin than a string bikini. Okay, maybe not as much, but pretty close. I've given a lot of thought about tonight, so I go with the one Austin would love and that will have Boone growling a wicked rumble in the back of his throat. He thinks no one can hear. I do and every time it makes me wet.

As for Landry, I can't tell for sure. He is a hard man to read, so I'll go with what two out of the three like.

I take a deep breath and let it out to a slow count of five, turning to see all the angles in the floor-length mirror. Braless in silk is as scandalous as it gets. While I'm at it, I go ahead and ditch the idea of using the white thong I have set out. With a dress this thin, why bother. I smile a little at what my bouncing breasts will do to all the sexual tension I plan on stoking to the max tonight. I have no intentions of leaving anything to anyone's imagination. If this doesn't get their dicks hard and my virginity taken tonight, I might just give up.

"It ain't getting any better, babe," I muse and fidget with my hair a little longer to get the blonde curls just right. I'm not a natural risk-taker, but it's time to throw all my built-in hesitation in the trash and let the wild girl in me out for the first time. My father always said I was wound too tight since birth, and I think I might have found the cure for that.

At least for an evening. And then I can go back to being the obedient daughter with the regal poise and perfect smile in the background.

Always in the background.

Usually, I have to be shoved into doing anything new, but tonight is my only chance to have them see me as more than the off-limits daughter of their high-profile client.

I want—need—them to see me as a woman. I tune out the white noise playing in my head telling me this won't end well.

Cool air kisses the bare, heated skin of my shoulders as I slip out of my bedroom and make my way down the hall. I descend the back stairs knowing I'll find Boone, Austin and Landry waiting for me. At the bottom of the stairs, I walk the short hall that spills into a large living area with plush sofas to the right and the spacious kitchen to the left.

I get to the halfway mark when I slow to a stop. I can already smell the combined scent of their cologne and feel a rush of excitement tingle in places I wish they would all touch, lick and nibble.

I've had a long time to think about this evening. Three years, in fact. Thirty-six torturous months of wondering, and dreaming, what it would be like to have all three of my bodyguards take me and give me all of my firsts. I know I'm untouchable. They've made that clear the few times I've dropped hints, but please God, have mercy on me this one time.

Every second of my life has been coordinated with events and an hourly schedule since my mother walked out on my father ten years ago. He doesn't talk about it, but I know he fills his days with endless meetings to drown the heartache which saddles me with all the more work as his personal assistant. Not a job I asked for, but naturally slipped into.

My father's need for structure and predictability has left our lives cold. Lifeless even and I'm tired of it. I've put off living my life long enough, so I'm taking back control from appointment books, calendars and a slew of digital screens taking over my life.

Lucky for me, my father is hosting a charity ball this evening and has stepped out early, leaving the house all to myself and my men. And since I control the schedule, I know we have two hours before I'm due at my father's side.

I slow toward the end of the hallway when I hear a masculine growl hit low in someone's throat. I can't tell who it is, but my money would be on Boone. He's always rambling on about one thing or another not going according to his plan.

I move to push forward, but Austin's words have me stopping in my tracks again, my shuffling steps silent on the thick carpet. I know it's wrong not to voice my presence, but I can't force myself to move.

"Get a damn grip, Austin."

I was right. Boone. My breath catches at the harshness I hear in his words. His voice is as rough around the edges as the man himself. Sure, he's mind-blowingly gorgeous, tall and clean-shaven, but he's also broody to the core and speaks more in growls than words at times.

He brushes the line of being ten years my senior and is the older of my three bodyguards by a year or two. He's also the one who forbids breaking protocol. Much to his annoyance, I enjoy pushing his buttons just to mess with him.

"How much longer are we going to wait? I seriously don't know if I can hold out much longer. Another week? Maybe. A month? I think that's pushing it. The little cock-tease has my balls bluer by the day."

Austin. The youngest of the group and the most laid-back man I've ever met. In a word, he's gorgeous but not in a polished never-get-dirty-kind of way. Smoky gray eyes, chiseled jawline and dark hair make him look every bit as off-limits as he seems.

"Good damn question none of us have an answer to and you know why. You're not the only one losing it."

That's Boone again. Clipped sentences mean he's getting irritated by the line of conversation.

"I don't know about you guys, but I dread seeing her tonight. My dick is going to be hard the whole time, and these pants are too tight to hide the hard-on I'll be sporting."

God above. Her? Her who? My heart quickens.

"Make that three of us."

Landry.

I close my eyes, processing everything I am hearing.

I would know his bourbon-and-smoke roughened voice in a crowd of a thousand people. Cool and calculated. My third bodyguard is just as perfectly built as the other two with broad, muscular shoulders and hard, hulking biceps. He towers over everyone by a good two inches and carries himself with an air of quiet confidence others lack. I've seen grown men cower under one of his hard glares, but he only makes me melt when he turns those dark green eyes my way. He's a gentle giant until some poor, unfortunate soul pisses him off or tries to get too close to me.

"What's the game plan again? Hell, do we even have one?"

Boone pauses.

"We're not talking about some bar hopping tag chaser looking for a quick one-nighter."

I almost slink back to my room, but as I turn to leave I'm brought up short by what Boone says next.

"She is off-limits. No game plan but to keep her safe. You know we all have to keep our hands and dicks to ourselves. I don't see that changing anytime soon either. Any of us act on the thoughts in our heads and we might as well kiss our careers goodbye, too. Especially Honor. The scandal it would bring on top of her would ruin the girl's life before she has a chance to really get started. You know I'm right."

I press a hand over my chest to try and calm my heavy breathing and racing heart at the sounds of my name mixed with the word dick and scandal on Boone's lips. All the doubt from before melts away, leaving a renewed resolve in its wake.

I smile.

"I know, damn it, we all do. You don't need to spell it out for me."

Landry this time. It takes a lot to get him agitated, and right now he sounds like a starved bear ready for a fight.

"Yeah, well, a good reminder doesn't hurt. Did you forget we all made a pact? No one goes near her unless we all do. Since that can't happen…"

Boone's words drop mid-sentence.

They are silent for another long pause that seems to drag on for eons until Landry speaks up.

"Do any of you know what she wants for her birthday?"

"That doesn't involve tying her to a bed and fucking her until none of us can walk?"

Boone grunts. "That's what we want."

Stunned, it's all I can do to stay on my feet much less keep up with who is saying what by now. I swallow a gasp at the sudden pool of heat soaking my thighs.

Holy shit.

Judging by how no one is speaking, none of them have an answer or they were all like me and imagining what me tied to a bed would look like.

Good thing for all of us I always come prepared.

I step around the corner and all eyes zero in on me with a burning fierceness. I blush.

Of course I blush.

I've never really done this kind of thing before. Come on to a pack of men, that is. Heat creeps up my neck, and I can feel my feet slowing, begging me to turn back, that this is a huge mistake, but I don't listen this time.

Sizzling fire in those eyes has me holding my breath as I cross the space between us.

Surprise from my bold actions pulls their brows high, but all three school their expressions into blank slates just as quickly.

Men. I practically roll my eyes.

Boone's piercing dark eyes burn into me, and I hold his hard look as I cross to where all three are standing. As I thought. The other two have bulges behind those zippers the second they eye my swaying, untamed tits, and candy hard nipples.

I have to give it to them. All stand unflinching and silent like stone sentinels.

With hard-ons.

Each man is dressed in a pristine white dress shirt neatly tucked into tailored black slacks with satin trim down the sides. Austin was right about his pants being too tight, for sure.

Landry and Austin's bowties hang untied around their necks, their jackets and weapon holsters are tossed over the barstools.

"You know," I draw out slowly for full effect and to make sure I have every ounce of their attention. "It's funny you boys should ask."

One tug and my dress pools around my feet in a puddle of blue silk.

Continue reading Honor for Three!

Read now on Amazon, Kindle Unlimited or print.

Welcome to the dark, twisted world of SONS OF BRATVA SAVAGES MC where both blood and demons run freely. The cost of patching into the brotherhood—your undying loyalty. But once in, you'll have a family for life.

Join the savage crew in this raw, gritty series where its hard, damaged members ride the line between darkness and light. Life and death. All seeking redemption from a life of sin through the strength of the strong women they come to love.

Sons of Bratva Savages:
Savage Justice
Savage Thief

ABOUT THE AUTHOR

Penelope Wylde loves playing on the dark side of romance, making her characters work for their happily-ever-after. Join her for a twisted ride through the gritty shadows before reaching the light. That is, if you dare to be WYLDE.

She writes overly possessive heroes and anti-heroes who are pure sinners at heart who bring enough heat to the pages to melt your hearts…and your panties. Billionaires, mafia, reverse harem, and bikers…the more forbidden the romance the more she loves to peel back the layers and discover what makes her characters tick.

She makes a wicked margarita mix, owns two hundred shades of red nail polish and is always found reading one forbidden romance or another when she's not writing.

www.PenelopeWylde.com

ALSO BY PENELOPE WYLDE

SONS OF BRATVA SAVAGES:

Savage Justice

Savage Thief

DARK REVERSE HAREM ROMANCE DUET:

Dark Mafia Kings

Dark Mafia Queen

HER FILTHY HAREM:

Her Filthy Professors

Her Filthy Mafia Men

Her Filthy Bratva Bodyguards

HAREM OF THREE:

Mercy for Three

Honor for Three

Justice for Three

CLUB SIN:

Room One

SAVAGE MOUNTAIN MEN:

Her Savage Mountain Man

Claimed by Her Mountain Man

Sharing Their Mountain Bride

His Snowbound Mountain Virgin

FORBIDDEN PROFESSORS:

The Professors' Sweet Treat

The Professor's Bought Bride

The Professor's Sweet Virgin

RED HOT SERIES:

Red Hot Christmas Virgin

Red Hot Naughty Vixen

Red Hot Dirty Bosses

HARD MEN IN UNIFORM:

Claimed by Her Soldier

Belonging to Her Soldier

DIRTY SECOND CHANCES:

Going Deep

Down On Me

In Too Deep

CHERRY POPPERS:

Cherry Sweet

Cherry Bossed

Cherrilicious Ink

Wild Cherry

MARRYING MY BILLIONAIRE BOSS DUET:

Claiming His Fake Bride 1

Claiming His Fake Bride 2

JINGLE SPELLS:

Jingle Spells #1

STANDALONES:

Unwrapping His Christmas Virgin

Dirty Little Blackmailer

Hard Riding

Rocked Deep

Doctor Babymaker

Eating Kandy

Wynter's Coming

Getting Screwged

Holly Kisses

202 Cherry Popper Way

706 Sugarbush Lane

Knocked Up by the Rock Star